| Chloe's Old Life | Chloe's New Life |
| --- | --- |
| Dirty clothes | Designer dresses |
| Broken washing machine | A maid and laundry service |
| Dingy, one-bedroom apartment | Three-room suite in a 130-room castle |
| Cantankerous, unreliable transport | Chauffered stretch limousine |
| Saturday nights with her dog, Friday | The best-looking, richest man in the world at her feet |

Now, if only Chloe can keep the kingdom from noticing she doesn't speak the Ennsway language, prefers blue jeans to silk skirts and won't marry for anything less than true love....

Dear Reader,

When Chloe Marshall met Princess Moira back in college, she never dreamed they'd one day be trading places. Imagine small-town girl Chloe in a 130-room castle with a maid, a stretch limo—and a gorgeous king hers for the asking!

And where has the real princess been all this time? Well, find out next month in #724 *Cowgirl in Pearls*, when Moira hooks up with the sexiest cowboy in the West!

We hope you enjoy this newest fun duet from popular author Jenna McKnight!

Jenna enjoys hearing from her readers. For a bookmark, send an SASE to P.O. Box 283, Grover, MO 63040-0283. Or e-mail her at Connections at the Harlequin/Silhouette web site at www.romance.net.

Happy reading!

Debra Matteucci
Senior Editor & Editorial Coordinator
Harlequin Books
300 East 42nd Street
New York, NY 10017

# *Princess in Denim*
## JENNA McKNIGHT

# *Harlequin Books*

TORONTO • NEW YORK • LONDON
AMSTERDAM • PARIS • SYDNEY • HAMBURG
STOCKHOLM • ATHENS • TOKYO • MILAN
MADRID • WARSAW • BUDAPEST • AUCKLAND

A special thank you to Emma Jensen for her patience and generosity, to Bonnie Crisalli for seeing the possibilities, to Debra Matteucci for understanding and, last but not least, to Huntley Fitzpatrick for jumping in.

ISBN 0-373-16719-9

PRINCESS IN DENIM

# *Prologue*

Chloe Marshall tugged a dirty tank top out of the hamper, sniffed it to make sure it wasn't totally unacceptable for wear, then slipped into it. One had to make concessions when the washing machine broke down. Again. It seemed all she'd done lately was make concessions.

She pulled her sun-bleached ponytail through the back of her Dodgers cap, grabbed a pair of toaster pop-ups for breakfast and her keys, then whistled up Friday, her black-and-white Australian shepherd. "Go for a ride?"

The dog tore through the run-down apartment in order to get to the door before Chloe could change her mind—as if she would. They'd been inseparable since they first laid eyes on each other at the dog pound three years ago; Chloe had learned not to take another job where she'd take home more than her paycheck.

Friday, stubby tail wagging and tongue hanging out, hogged the driver's seat of Chloe's army-surplus jeep.

"Move over. You know you can't drive."

Chloe slipped in behind the wheel, coaxed the vintage vehicle to start one more time, whispered a quick "Thank you" to the powers that be and headed north, away from Santa Barbara. Friday kept her brown eyes steadfastly on Chloe until she'd devoured all but the last crumb of her strawberry pop-ups, which she shared.

Rancho Santa Ynez, a quaint, private little rancho with low stucco buildings and red-tiled roofs, nestled snugly in the Santa Ynez Mountains. Chloe couldn't afford to keep a horse there herself, but she bartered her equine skills for riding time.

She tapped her horn to warn the barn cats that she'd brought their worst enemy, then parked next to her best friend Moira's limo. Friday leaped out and took up her vigilant post as man's best friend and feline eradicator. Though if the dog ever caught one, Chloe wasn't sure just what she'd do with it.

"Morning, John."

Moira's driver paced a slow circle around the shiny black limo. He had a rolled up newspaper in one hand, and he tipped his head respectfully in Chloe's direction. "Miss Marshall."

It was John's job to drive Moira to the rancho and wait for her. It was his passion to prevent the cats from adorning the limo's spotless sheen with pawprints. Now that Chloe was here and Friday had sent the cats scurrying for the rafters, John could take a break.

"Have you been here long?"

"Twelve and a half minutes, to be exact."

John was always exact. Moira's whole staff, as a matter of fact, was exact. Unequaled. Perfect in every way.

Which only highlighted the foibles in Chloe's everyday existence. The broken washing machine. The cranky Jeep. The dented front bumper that hadn't been her fault.

"Chloe!" Moira yelled from inside the barn. "Come get this mutt away from me."

"See you later, John."

Everyone else steered clear of Chloe's dog, and vice versa. Moira, however, was a princess—for real—in spite of being Chloe's best friend. And Her Royal Highness, the Princess Moira of Ennsway, didn't have it in her to give the shepherd a wide berth and ignore the perpetual growls.

"Hi, Moira." With a simple wave of her hand, Chloe dispersed Friday to the other end of the barn before Moira had a hissy fit.

"Who're you riding today?"

Chloe didn't get her pick of whom she rode; it was determined by the number of hours she'd worked. And the drudge scale. Graining at dawn bartered a better mount than, say, graining in the evening. And a week of mucking out stalls gave her two hours' use of the owner's prize stallion.

Chloe hadn't earned anything this week. "Bum's Henry."

Moira snickered. "Really, Chloe, Doc's wasting a good equestrian like you on Hank."

"Yeah, I know, but I had a test in geology *and* a paper in psych this week, so you know I didn't get much real work done. It's okay, though. Hank reminds me of the first mustang I caught and broke."

Moira got a dreamy look on her face. Chloe suspected it had nothing to do with the fact that some poor lackey was tacking up Moira's Lipizzan for her. A princess, after all, didn't have to do anything on a drudge scale. She got to sit cross-legged on a bale of sweet alfalfa and wait patiently. Now, if a genie suddenly appeared and granted Chloe three wishes, that one sounded like a pretty good start. But that was about as likely to happen as her lottery numbers all coming up on the same day.

"A real mustang?"

"Uh-huh." In the stall, Chloe had to squeeze into a corner with Hank, a bay gelding, just to get the halter on the opinionated beast. She started to lead him out, and Friday ran in to nip at his heels, just in case he didn't feel up to a workout today. No one was surprised when Hank bolted through the door, barely missing Chloe's feet, which was entirely due to her quick reflexes and not his "sparkling" personality.

"You're so lucky," Moira said.

Chloe tripped over her own feet. "Excuse me?"

"Well, look at you."

Chloe checked out her unwashed tank top, her faded jeans and her cowboy boots, which were so old, they had stories to tell. "Yeah, so?"

Moira lowered her voice. "You live by yourself. You drive by yourself. You can cover a bad hair day with a ball cap—"

"I always wear a ball cap."

Moira smiled apologetically. "I know. I didn't mean anything by it. I just meant if you *had* a bad hair day, no one would notice."

"Uh-huh." She'd never heard her friend quite like this. "And this is leading where?"

Moira sighed as Chloe hooked Hank in the cross ties and applied the mud scraper and a good deal of elbow grease to his coat. "I dreamed about the castle last night."

Chloe perked up. Moira used to tell such wonderful stories about the castle where she'd grown up—an actual bailey, a great hall, a staff that outnumbered a small city, birthday parties with elephants to ride...

"I'm surprised I dreamed about it. I don't miss it at all."

Chloe did, and she'd never set foot in Ennsway, or any other part of Europe. "Tell me about it," she begged.

"My dream?"

"Your castle."

And so, while Chloe scraped crust off Hank, Moira rewove fairy tales about her childhood—a stable full of prize horses, Christmas gifts of porcelain dolls and diamond bracelets from heads of state, a canopied bed in a room big enough to house an orchestra....

Emma, Moira's private secretary, perched herself on a nearby bale of hay. She was a tall, slender woman, smartly dressed in a chambray suit that earned its price tag by looking deceptively casual. "If you miss it so much, we can go home," she said softly.

Moira shot to her feet. "But I don't!" She paced the dirt-packed aisle. "I never have. Chloe, remember when we used to trade places with each other?"

Chloe darted a glance at Emma. Sure, it was a little late now to worry about getting caught, but they'd never told anyone. Or at least *she* hadn't.

"Oh, she knows." Moira's laugh was light and carefree. "She had us figured out all along."

"Yeah, I remember." With Hank clean and his hooves picked, Chloe started to tack up. She looked forward to these rides, and wanted to get on the Santa Ynez trails as soon as possible. It wasn't punching cattle in Texas. It wasn't trick riding in rodeos. But on the mountain trails, all her problems melted away for an hour or two. "As I recall, I got the better end of the deal."

"You think?"

"Sure. I got Emma, the chauffeur, the maid, the nice clothes, meals which I still can't pronounce the names of—"

"How would you like to do it again?"

"What?"

Moira checked over her shoulder and lowered her voice. "How would you like to trade places again?"

Chloe grinned. "You have some prince coming to court you that you don't want?"

"I'm serious."

"So am I. Throw in a prince and you've got a deal." When that got no response, Chloe peeked over Hank's withers at Moira and Emma. The two women were standing as near to side by side as they could get, keeping in mind Emma's subservient position. "You're serious?"

"Deadly."

"But we only did it years ago to fool the profs. You're not even in school anymore."

It was Moira's turn to grin. "Well, *some* of us have to graduate. Unlike you, who just keeps on learning."

"I could graduate."

"You have enough credits for four degrees."

"What can I say? I like college."

Chloe didn't catch Moira's mutter, but it sounded suspiciously like "I guess."

Chloe's mind raced with imagined delights. Maybe Moira needed a substitute for a grand ball. There was nothing wrong with a weekend of chauffeur-driven limousine rides, wearing a long gown and dripping in diamonds. She'd never seen Moira with a tiara; maybe one of those was too much to wish for.

"Who would we be fooling? And for how long?"

There was a moment of total silence, a rather rare thing in a barn. No dog barking at a cat, no horse stomping its irritation with a fly. Just one woman waiting for an answer that was slow in coming from two others.

"Everyone," Moira finally answered. "Forever."

"Yeah, I wish. April Fool's was last month."

"We're serious, Chloe," Emma said. The fact that she'd joined the conversation and included herself with that "we" gave Chloe her first hint that she'd been set up.

"Serious?" Chloe tightened Hank's girth and snickered. "Uh-huh."

Moira stepped closer and faced Chloe across the seat of the western saddle. "Honest to God, Chloe. We're serious."

Chloe looked her in the eyes. She'd known Moira for ten years. In all that time, Moira had never teased her mercilessly, which was what Chloe feared this might be. "You know, it wouldn't be nice for y'all to tempt me with an offer like this and then yank it back out of my reach."

Expectation lightened Moira's smile. "You'll consider it, then?"

*A chauffeur, a maid, a chef, a private secretary, a castle in Ennsway...*

What was not to consider?

"Nah. Y'all are loco if you think we'd get away with it. There are too many people here who know us."

"Not here," Moira said quickly. "My father wants

me to come home to stay. No one in Ennsway has seen me since I was twelve.''

Chloe heard hope in Moira's voice, desperation, as if she were a hungry animal sensing that its prey will tire before it does. It was reaffirmed by Moira's quickening speech.

''We fooled all of our professors, Chloe. Some of our classmates. You liked being treated like a princess—you said so every time. We can *do* this, Chloe. I know we can. And...and Emma will go home with you. You know, to help you over the rough spots. Say you'll do it, Chloe. Please.''

Who in her right mind would say no?

# Chapter One

*How I Spent My Spring Break...by Chloe Marshall.*

Chloe pulled her ponytail through her blue-and-white ball cap and amended that to *How I Spent the Rest of My Life as a Princess...* The "by" part got her on that one. *Would* it be by Chloe Marshall? Or, having spent the past week learning princess rules and wearing princess clothes and practicing princess things, it probably should be *by Princess Moira.*

But she wasn't feeling a hundred percent royal just yet. Not because she was tired from a long day of getting ready, but because the reality just hadn't sunk in. She'd gone over and over the plan, looking for a catch. But, knowing Moira as well as she did, she wasn't surprised to find none.

"Friday! Come on, girl. Time to go."

After a week of round-the-clock intensive trading-places study in Moira's cliffside condo, Chloe's apartment looked even more worn. Everything that hadn't been sold or given away was packed. Moira was moving on, and wouldn't be taking Chloe's place here. They were both leaving California behind, a part of their past never to be revisited.

And, as she'd thought a couple of times this past

week, she wondered how she was going to get over moving away from her best friend. It wasn't as if Moira could fly to Ennsway for a visit; that would be tempting fate. As a royal princess, Chloe wouldn't be able to just hop a jet and move in with Moira for the weekend, wherever she ended up; Chloe would have an entire entourage to account for.

She took one last look around the apartment. No, last week it had been worn. This week it was shabby. She lugged out three pieces of mismatched luggage, closed the door and led the way toward a taxi. Her confused dog followed closely.

"I don't like dogs in my cab," the driver said bluntly.

Friday growled ominously, and the short, round man backed off slowly, then made a dash for his place behind the wheel. He turned the key, shifted into drive and promptly killed the engine. Fortunately for Chloe, who was then able to throw her luggage into the back seat and jump in after it before the cabbie could leave her standing on the curb.

"Santa Barbara Airport," she told him, and hoped he was listening.

Friday, who'd leaped into the cab with her, rested her head on the back of the front seat and growled every time the poor man glanced her way. By the time they reached the airport, he had beads of sweat popping out on his neck.

He scurried out his door, opened the back one and reached in tentatively. Friday apparently decided it was her job to keep this man from robbing Chloe of her few possessions, and escalated her growls accordingly.

"Come on, lady, gimme a break."

"Oh, now you're talking to me?"

She snapped the brand-new leash onto the brand-new collar, her going-away present to her second-best friend. Before she knew it, she was standing on the sidewalk beside her luggage as the cab sped away, tires squealing.

"But wait, sir, I forgot your tip," she said airily. "Come on, girl."

Friday wasn't accustomed to a leash, and Chloe wasn't very handy with three bags and a leashed dog who had her hog-tied in eight seconds. On the ninth second, Chloe hit the pavement. A nice young man in a business suit stepped forward to help, and the dog scared him into backing off.

About this time, with Chloe wrapped up on her rear on the pavement, Moira's limo pulled up. Her baggage master whisked her luggage away. Moira waited for John to open the door for her and then emerged in a beautiful pale yellow jacket-and-skirt ensemble that would have cost Chloe six months' pay. It was topped off with a pearl necklace and matching earrings that were undoubtedly real and of the finest quality. Not that Chloe would know, except that she knew Moira only got the best. Emma saw to that. They immediately headed toward the terminal entrance.

"Uh, hel-lo-o…" Chloe said, when no one seemed to notice her sitting there. She tried to get up, but she hadn't gotten untangled yet.

Emma's jaw dropped open, and then she closed her eyes, as if not looking would assure her the whole week's worth of princess tutoring hadn't been wasted.

Moira's regal look gave way to a grin. "Hello, your-self. Teddy, see to Miss Marshall's bags, too, please."

Teddy jumped to do her bidding. "Yes, Your Royal Highness."

"I'd have someone help you up, Chloe, but nobody can get near you with that mongrel growling like that."

Chloe ignored her friend's smirk. "Hey, she's pure-bred. And she doesn't bite."

"How would you know?"

"She's never bitten anyone." Chloe unhooked the leash from Friday's collar—it was the only way she could get unwound. Moira and Emma immediately looked anywhere but *at* the dog, knowing that aggravated her, until Chloe was on her feet and reattached.

Moira looked at the leash pointedly. "I didn't know you knew how to use one of those things."

Chloe chuckled. "If I did, I wouldn't have been sitting on the sidewalk."

As they walked side by side through the arched doorway into the Spanish-style terminal, Moira lowered her voice and asked, "Did you remember everything?"

Chloe glanced around to make sure no one would hear. "Mmm-hmm. Operation Fairy Tale has commenced. Or did we decide to call it Operation Grass Is Greener on the Other Side—?"

Moira snickered. "Quit before you make me laugh."

"What's wrong with laughing?" Had she forgotten something? She really had to get all these rules straight. "Don't princesses laugh in public?"

"We don't want to draw attention to ourselves today."

"Uh, gee, Moira, I think I already did that with that swan dive I did outside. Where're you going? The ticket counter's over there."

Arched eyebrows told her better than words ever could have that Princess Moira didn't do ticket counters.

"Oh."

"This way, Your Royal Highness, Miss Marshall," Emma advised them softly.

Emma had called Chloe by her first name for the past nine years. It unnerved Chloe to hear her get so formal now. She knew it was because they were in a public place, but it was just one more reminder that her life was changing. She just hoped it was going forward, not in reverse.

"Princess Moira!" a man yelled.

Moira didn't look, but Chloe did, out of curiosity. In the nick of time, Emma held up her pocketbook and blocked the photographer's aim.

"Don't let anyone get your picture, Chloe," Moira whispered.

And then Chloe understood. No one in Ennsway had seen the princess in sixteen years. If either of them got their picture splashed in a newspaper, their whole plot could be in jeopardy. Not that anyone would splash Chloe's picture anywhere. She was just a California blonde wearing a ball cap, a short jacket, and jeans. Not a photo op that would earn anyone a paycheck.

As instructed, Chloe put her hand up to the side of her face as the camera flashed repeatedly, until John and Teddy performed their last outgoing-staff function and blocked the photographer's progress. Even then, Chloe worried about a long-distance paparazzo catching them. It would be a shame to have come this far, to have sold all her possessions, just to call it all off at the last minute because of an ambitious photographer.

Being a princess had definite advantages. Chloe, Moira, and Emma weren't stopped by anyone, but were promptly escorted out to the private jet awaiting them.

"We're almost there," Moira encouraged her.

"Good. I brought my notes with me so I can go over

them again on the plane. I have a couple questions already.''

Moira led the way up the steps, followed by Emma, followed by Chloe. As she boarded the plane, a dark-haired man in a conservative brown suit and tie stepped forward, bowed and introduced himself to Moira.

''I am Humphrey, Your Royal Highness. I will bring you up-to-date on all the changes in Ennsway since you've been gone.'' He sounded quite stuffy, and when he glanced down his nose at Emma, it was clear he thought she was on her way out.

Chloe remained behind Emma's back and kept her face averted. If this guy was a member of the new staff, she and Moira had to trade places immediately, before he got a good look at either of them. She pulled the bill on her ball cap lower over her eyes, and Moira left her sunglasses on.

''Your brother hired me especially for you, as your private secretary.''

*Private secretary.* What the heck did he think Emma was?

Chloe cleared her throat—the only way she dared signal her distress at this point. If Emma suddenly dropped out of the picture, Chloe was going back home. There was no way she could fly to a foreign country and masquerade as its royal princess without Emma's round-the-clock help. It would be a bit complicated to slip back into the old life she'd shed like a snakeskin this past week. But it could be done. Perhaps her neighbor wouldn't mind returning the rocking chair she'd given her; who needed to rock a new baby, anyway? Perhaps her landlord hadn't already found another renter. Perhaps she could get her jeep back without paying a ridiculous penalty.

Yeah. Right.

"Emma is my private secretary, Humphrey," Moira said, in a tone that Chloe hadn't been able to master after an entire semester of Assertiveness Training 101.

"Your Royal Highness," Humphrey continued, "if I may point out that she has been away from Ennsway for sixteen years... It would make more sense if she stayed on as *my* assistant."

Chloe swore she could hear her heart thumping faster than a cornered jackrabbit's. *Go, Moira.*

"Assistant will be a fine position for you, if you want it, Humphrey."

"But, Your Royal Highness—"

"I'll hear no more about it, Humphrey." Moira moved to brush past him, and he jumped out of her way.

Emma followed Moira, and Chloe followed her without hesitation, still keeping her face averted. She knew they breezed past the staff, but didn't dare look up to see who they were. She'd meet them later—as Her Royal Highness, the Princess Moira of Ennsway.

"One more thing, Your Royal Highness—" Humphrey said.

Moira didn't look back; none of them did.

"His Royal Majesty, the King of Baesland, is tending business in the city. He will return to the plane momentarily."

Chloe was certain the three women couldn't avoid the neighboring king as handily as they had the staff. There would be little or no time to review her notes as planned. She could turn around right now, run out the door of the plane, down the steps, across the tarmac and back through the terminal. She could beg her landlord for her apartment back—at the new rate, if need be. She could get another job and return to classes.

She could go back to wearing dirty clothes out of the hamper, stand in line at the bank only to find out she was overdrawn, and muck out stalls until her calluses had calluses.

*No way!*

THE PRIVATE JET was from Baesland, the neighboring country to Moira's Ennsway, compliments of His Royal Majesty, the king. In it was a private bedroom. Not just an ordinary bedroom, either. One with solid cherrywood walls, gold light fixtures, a king-size bed, and plush Oriental throw rugs; a full-size bathroom of marble, with gold faucets on the sink and shower, and crystal decanters on the vanity that held anything a visitor, such as Princess Moira, was likely to want.

"Wow," Chloe whispered in awe. "I'll bet 'Lifestyles' would like to see this."

And apparently it also came with a maid, as one knocked at the door and hovered there, waiting for permission to enter.

Chloe heard well-bred exasperation in Moira's sigh and wondered if she could duplicate it in the days and weeks to come.

"Leave us," Moira said.

And the maid vanished, just like that. Chloe wished she'd been able to get rid of a few dates that easily.

"Lock the door behind me," Emma suggested. "I'll be back in fifteen minutes to check you two out."

Chloe locked the door behind her, then whirled on Moira. "You didn't tell me there'd be a king on board."

Moira unwove her French braid, and none too

gently. "I didn't know. Come on, hurry up. You don't want to keep him waiting when he gets here. It'll be your first test."

"*First* test? What do you call that gauntlet we just ran through?"

Moira dismissed that with a wave of her hand. Chloe tried it, too, just to see if she could get the same effect.

"What are you doing?" Moira asked with a laugh.

Chloe grinned good-naturedly. "Practicing being you."

"Don't worry about it. It's better if you're just you. Anything you do will be all right."

Chloe muttered, "I'll believe that when I see it," and whipped off her ball cap.

They traded everything except their underwear. Chloe got the designer sunglasses, Moira got the Dodgers cap and ponytail. Chloe got the pearls and pale yellow silk suit, Moira the jacket and jeans; the skirt was a little short on Chloe, and Moira got her first lesson in making cuffs. They'd known ahead of time that Chloe couldn't fit into Moira's shoes, so Chloe dug in her backpack for her outrageously expensive new pair of pumps, and Moira stuffed tissues in the toes of the scruffy cowboy boots.

"Ready?" Moira asked.

"Ready. What do we do now?"

Chloe stood still as Moira appraised her.

"You need mascara."

"I don't wear mascara."

"You do now."

"But you said I should just be myself."

"Well, yourself wears mascara today. And blush."

A knock sounded at the door.

"It's probably Emma. I'll get it," Chloe said as she turned toward the door.

"No!"

Chloe stopped dead in her tracks.

"Jeez, Chloe, you're a royal princess now. Act like it," Moira snapped. And she stomped across the floor, checked to see that it was Emma, and let her in.

Chloe was speechless. Moira had turned into her—Chloe—faster and easier than Chloe was managing to turn into a princess. She had to get her act together.

Emma hovered by Moira's side as she examined Chloe. "She needs makeup."

"I know," Moira answered. "But fifteen minutes ago, I was a princess who didn't carry any."

"Ah." Emma handed over her purse. "Go for it."

Still fretting over the king, Chloe asked, "Is he here yet?"

"His secretary just phoned. His Majesty is on the way."

"Relax, Chloe…uh, Moira," Moira said. "He'll be happy to see you. He's an old family friend."

Just what she needed—someone who'd known Moira as she used to be. Someone who knew the family well. Someone who, if he discovered the deception, might feel honorbound to toss her off the airplane.

Chloe slumped onto the padded stool by the vanity. "Great. Do I jump plane now, or wait for him to throw me out?"

Moira shoved a mascara wand into Chloe's hand and turned her to face the mirror. "Make yourself look like a princess, kid."

"He'd better have poor eyesight."

"You've been my best friend for ten years. Just act like me—in your own way, of course."

A messenger tapped on the door, and Emma spoke with him. "His Royal Majesty has just arrived," she told Chloe and Moira.

Chloe looked in the mirror. Other than mildly petrified, she looked pretty darned good with a touch of mascara, blush and lipstick. Maybe, if Baesland had a prince, and the king didn't see through her disguise, he'd take a liking to her looks and send the prince her way. She missed her ponytail and ball cap, though.

"Remember, *Moira,* act regal."

THE LONG SILVER-GRAY LIMO oozed luxury. Its seats were of the softest silver-gray leather, matching carpet lay underfoot and up the doors, Yanni drifted softly out of invisible speakers, the bar was well stocked and, just in case an occupant wanted to work instead of relax, a computer, fax, and phone were discreetly cabineted away.

His Royal Majesty, King William, noticed none of it. "Leonard."

As always, William's private secretary responded promptly, "Yes, Your Majesty?"

"Send a follow-up letter to the surgeon in Los Angeles, thanking him for the appointment today and detailing what we discussed. I would like him to respond as soon as possible."

"And Mr. Edwards at UCSB?"

"Yes, the same. Restate the urgency of breaking ground this year. And mention that I am deeply grateful for his meeting me at such a late hour. I am certain that was quite unusual for him."

"Yes, Your Majesty." Leonard's normal mask broke into the slightest of grins. "I'd say the six cups of coffee he consumed were evidence of that."

For the first time in his life, William checked his tie—the red power tie that his valet had deemed appropriate for today's meetings. It had a crown woven into it, so subtly that people consciously did not see it, but subconsciously were constantly faced with the fact that he was a king, and they were not. It was fine for a day of business appointments, but not for greeting the princess.

"Damn." He loosened the knot and yanked it off.

"What, Your Majesty?"

"Is she there?"

"Yes, Your Majesty. She boarded the plane fifteen minutes ago." He deftly caught the tie as William threw it aside. "I'll find you another."

William gave the matter little thought. "Better not."

"But, Your Majesty, you never—"

"If she is as spineless as the rest of her family, I do not wish to scare her. I only want to make a good impression."

"Very well." Leonard draped it over his shoulder. "I will keep it handy for your appointment in Texas."

If Leonard said more, William did not notice. The luxuriousness of the limo eluded him, not because he was used to it—he was—but because his mind was on the princess he had not seen in sixteen years. She had been a child to him, when she was twelve and he eighteen. Reserved and well mannered. Not beautiful, but—what was the American expression? Ah, yes, *cute.*

"We're almost there, Your Majesty." Leonard's voice carried an undercurrent that spoke volumes. *Sit back, relax, take a deep breath. You are the king, she is just a princess.*

William tried it for ten seconds; it did not work.

Leonard had been with him forever. If he could talk to anybody, it should be he.

"How do I look?"

Leonard took his time assessing His Majesty from head to toe, and William grew impatient.

"She is used to Americans, you know, Leonard. They are quite relaxed, I think. Do I look relaxed?"

"You might loosen your collar, Your Majesty."

William undid the top two buttons of his dress shirt. "Should I take off my jacket?"

"You look quite dashing in it."

William grinned. "Dashing, hmm? That is good."

"Very good, Your Majesty. Then, when her father announces the good news about the upcoming nuptials—"

"Remember not to— How do the Americans say it? Do not let the cat slip?"

"Out of the bag."

"Yes, do not let the cat out of the bag. A most strange expression. Who keeps a cat in a bag?" Before Leonard could reply, William continued, "I wish to develop a friendship with her first."

"Yes, Your Majesty. Maybe even romance her a bit. Then she will see how fortunate she is to be getting you."

William took a deep breath and relaxed back against the leather. "Yes, she is."

CHLOE HAD LIVED the past ten years in Santa Barbara, home to many highly paid movie stars who yearned for a slower-paced life-style in which to raise their families. A slower pace, however, didn't mean they left their jewels in Hollywood. Chloe had seen pearls adorning some of the women. Never, though, had she thought to have a string of these well-matched babies around her own neck.

"Don't fidget. Leave them alone," Emma ordered, and Chloe obediently dropped her hands.

"Here's the purse," Moira said as she handed the soft leather bag—navy to match the trim on the jacket collar and pumps—to Chloe.

It weighed no more than a feather. Chloe opened it and peeked inside. "A tissue? You carry a purse just so you have a tissue?"

Moira's eyebrows arched humorously. "Like, what do I need, huh?"

Chloe had never heard Moira speak so...casually, and it made her laugh. "Pretty good, Moira."

"Chloe. You've got to remember to call me Chloe."

Chloe pulled herself up straighter, as if she had a string attached to the top of her head to make her taller. She tucked the purse next to her ribs and held it with her arm. She touched the pearls to be sure they were still there, then remembered to leave them alone. "You're absolutely right, Chloe, dear." She turned to face her new private secretary and almost got the giggles. "Emma, I'm ready to meet His Majesty now."

"I'll just wait for y'all in here," Moira drawled in the exaggerated Texas accent that Chloe had lost years ago.

Chloe grabbed her by the hand. "Over my dead body."

Moira tugged free. "No, really, I'm serious. This is your presentation. You do this. I'll be out later, and Emma can introduce me as Chloe Marshall. Just remember one thing."

"What?"

"If I can do you, you can do me. I'll be American,

and you don't be sassy to His Majesty if you don't like him.''

"Me? Sassy?''

Moira rolled her eyes. "Oh, puh-lease.''

Chloe swallowed a laugh. Yes, she was sassy at times. She hadn't grown up in the wilds of Texas, with foster siblings who came and went with great irregularity, and not learned to stand up for herself come hell or high water.

Emma opened the door. Chloe took a deep breath and walked through it, right into her new life. Right out to meet a man who was supposed to be an old family friend with poor eyesight, and instead turned out to be a fairy-tale prince in a charcoal gray suit.

William stood near the door, quietly giving orders to his secretary, the pilot, and a handful of other people. Chloe watched in fascination as they jumped even faster for him than Moira's staff did for her—and she'd thought *they* were quick.

When the others noticed Chloe's approach, so did he. Tall, he could see over their heads. Dark, he met California's beach standards for tan, with his hair a rich black that Prince Charming would have killed for. Not a hint of gray at the temples. Handsome, without being pretentious; lapis eyes—Chloe knew that color from her Egyptian art class—straight nose, white teeth behind a slightly crooked smile.

Then, suddenly, a frown that mirrored Chloe's thoughts.

This might be an old family friend, but he wasn't *that* old. He didn't even wear glasses. Not so much as a squint. How well had he known Moira when she was twelve? And would he notice a difference now?

She heard Emma's voice as if it were far off. "Your Royal Majesty..."

Chloe stood frozen to the carpet as the introduction continued.

*I'm Moira. I'm Moira.* Maybe if she repeated it enough, she'd remember it.

"...Her Royal Highness, the Princess Moira," Emma finished.

Chloe forced a pleasant smile and tried to remember what she was supposed to do now. Curtsy? Bow? Shake his hand? The mere thought of touching his hand made hers sweat.

William stepped forward, his frown hardening to a glare as he peered down at her. "You cannot be Moira," he boomed.

Chloe dropped the purse. Her stomach plummeted to her ankles. She struggled to remember the definition of treason and wondered, if she'd just committed it, what the punishment would be.

She could pick up the purse, stalling for time until she figured out what to do. Or she could act like a royal princess.

Well, how to do that eluded her just this moment.

It was on the tip of her tongue to ask *Why the hell not?* but Moira had told her not to be sassy to the king.

So what was an American-blooded, foreign princess to do?

# Chapter Two

Emma plucked the fallen purse off the carpet before Chloe could think coherently enough to get her own knees to bend. Of course, she shouldn't be picking up her own purse, anyway, but old habits died hard. Her next-best bet was to open her mouth and see what came out—even sassy would be better than a mere squeak—but her voice disappeared completely when William's large hands got a firm grip on her arms just below the shoulders.

*Oh, God, he's fixin' to throw me off the plane.*

The slightly crooked grin William had displayed just moments ago appeared again, transforming his face, tugging answering smiles from the others around him. Except Chloe. She was still too uncertain of her near future.

"You are far too grown-up to be Moira. Last time I saw you, you were a little girl!"

She hadn't known she was holding her breath until necessity forced her to gasp in a fresh supply of oxygen. Which whooshed right back out again when William, his hands still firmly on her, dipped his head.

*Oh, God...*

His lips grazed first one cheek, then the other, in a

touch so soft, so warm, so gentle, yet solid enough that she knew she'd been kissed. By a king who wasn't a relative or a nearsighted old man, but one hell of a hunk.

Oh, not a kiss meant to buckle her knees and set her heart racing in anticipation. But, all the same, it did.

"Your Majesty."

Was that her whispering? She thought it was, but this was all so unreal. Apparently, she'd just passed the first crucial step. She felt a jab in her back; Emma was punishing her for fidgeting with the pearls again. She lowered her hand, hunted for pockets in which to trap them both, and found she had none.

"Mr. Richmond." William addressed the pilot, but his eyes never left Chloe, which didn't give her a second to reconnoiter. "We are ready to leave. Steward, I did not get your name…"

"Stephen, Your Majesty."

"Stephen, you may serve dinner as soon as we are in the air."

"Yes, Your Majesty."

Chloe listened as the orders went on in the king's precise speech pattern. Fly. Dinner—she'd forgotten to eat all day; she wasn't sure whether the ache in her stomach was nerves or hunger. Coffee. Call ahead to Texas. See to Her Highness's guest. Sit here.

"Oh," Chloe said with surprise when she realized he meant her. If his waving hand was any indication of his intent, he was indicating the chair right next to his. "Here?"

"Yes, sit by me. We can catch up while we dine."

The seating far exceeded any domestic first class section Chloe had ever seen on her way through a plane to coach. There were no rows of seats, but informal groupings of chairs upholstered in a green so rich it rivaled malachite; no tray tables to lower, but, once they were in the air, a real table that was whisked up in front of them, locked into place and draped with a snowy white cloth; crystal glasses etched with an intricate design that probably represented the monarchy, but Chloe couldn't show her ignorance by asking; fine china, gold flatware, and burgundy cloth napkins.

If Chloe had been given a typical airline choice of entrées, she would've been at a loss to make a decision. Her head was still reeling. Food appeared in front of her, and she ate it without noticing as she wondered—and worried—what questions the king would ask that could trip her up.

William snapped his fingers, and Chloe jumped in surprise. The steward jumped, too, not from surprise, but to get more coffee.

"You are very quiet," William said. "Is everything all right?"

She was surrounded by people filling her coffee cup, her stemmed water goblet, her wineglass, when what she really wanted was for William to stop staring at her.

"Yes," she answered. When he didn't return to his own food, she hastily tacked on, "Really. I'm fine."

She felt like a bug under a microscope, but she couldn't tell him that. She was supposed to be used to this kind of treatment from the staff, used to dining with a king. After all, her father was the king of Ennsway. As for the way William stared at her, could she do the same to him? He was a king, yes, but not her sovereign. He ruled the country next door, not her.

This etiquette business was impossible to remember. She'd just have to get Emma or Moira alone and ask.

And she'd sit by herself later and study her notes again.

"Telephone call, Your Majesty. From Dr. Lowenstein in Texas."

"Thank you, Leonard. Excuse me, please, Your Highness. I will not bore you with my business call."

Chloe breathed a big sigh of relief as he left the table. She could handle "More water, Your Highness?" better than "When *was* the last time we saw each other?"

William turned back to her for just a moment. "Oh, remind me when I get back, I have a message for you from your brother. He is most eager to see you again."

"MY BROTHER... My brother..." Chloe muttered to herself as she leafed through the pages of notes she'd written the past week, looking for any information she had on a sibling. She'd hidden the notes safely in her jeans pocket, which Moira was now wearing, and retrieved them under protest.

In a nearby chair, Moira inched her hand out toward Friday and, with a pasted-on smile, said, "Come on, you stupid mutt. We're going to be roommates. Let me pet you." The dog would have none of it, and maintained a continuous low, rumbling protest.

For the life of her, Chloe couldn't find much on her supposed brother. Did her life depend on it? What did they do with treasonists these days? And their look-alike accomplices? If she appeared less than she was supposed to be to King William, would he confide his suspicions to Moira's father? Would she end up in a dungeon, or was that too archaic? And, even if it was, who would protest? Moira was descended from a true monarch with the power to rule his subjects as he saw fit, not a royal figurehead who had to answer to anyone else.

"Why don't I have anything on my brother?" she whispered to Moira. She was proud of herself for getting the "my" part correct. "What's his name?" She flipped another page. "Ah, Louis, here he is."

"Chlo— Moira, be careful," Moira whispered back. "You can't go flashing those pages around. It'll give us away."

"Don't worry. Everyone's watching you and the dog."

"Not me. Just the mutt."

"I told you, she's pure—"

"Yeah, yeah, I know what you said. But I think it's a look-alike masquerading as an Aussie. A Border collie mix with its tail whacked off." Moira sniffed her uppity little royal nose. "No purebred acts so bitchy."

Chloe snickered. "You're saying you never act bitchy?"

"Of course not."

"Get real. Here's what I've got. His name is Louis. He's two years younger than you—"

"You."

"Yeah, me. And you said he's out of the country ninety-nine percent of the time." Chloe shot her soon-to-be-*ex*-friend a stern look. "So what's he doing 'waiting eagerly' to see me again?"

"One percent?"

Chloe glared at her, but Moira had been a princess too long to be intimidated by an amateur.

"Don't sweat it." Moira grabbed Chloe's notes and tore them in half.

Shock slowed Chloe down too much for her to grab them back before all that remained were little bits and pieces. She opened her mouth to protest about how she was supposed to remember everything without a cheat sheet, but only a squeak came out.

"It's too risky," Moira explained. "Now, as to Louis, he was only ten when I left. You shouldn't have any trouble convincing him you're me. Just stick your nose up in the air and pretend you're too good for him."

Chloe'd had foster brothers from time to time; nothing permanent, as this would be. What would a ten-year-old boy remember about his big sister sixteen years later? Not much, she was certain. So he was going to end up being her little brother until the day she died. Could be nice, if they got off to a friendly start and if Moira hadn't treated him insufferably.

"You didn't pick on him a lot when he was little, did you?"

"Of course not. We barely saw each other and, when we did, we behaved like proper little royals."

Chloe wasn't sure she believed that; she'd known Moira too long. "Proper little royals" didn't fool college professors by trading places with their best friends.

WILLIAM'S MIND was only half on his phone call, his very important business call with a Dallas surgeon he wanted to recruit for the new hospital staff. He was sequestered behind a jade-and-mother-of-pearl wall screen, but, if he cocked his head to the right just a little, he could see through the narrow gap between two of the panels.

Moira had moved to sit by her friend—Chloe, he thought her name was, a nice-looking American girl who did not know how to dress. Unlike Moira, whose hair shone in an elegant French braid, whose makeup was sheer enough to let her true beauty show through, and whose suit was of the finest pale yellow silk. It hugged her curves without fitting like a second skin, just hinting at the woman beneath.

A man's voice barked through the phone receiver and into William's ear, drawing him reluctantly back to the business at hand. "Yes, Doctor, yes, I am still here. Sorry."

He really had to keep his mind on business. The future of his country depended on it.

Her eyes were hazel, with gold and green flecks. He could not see them from where he was now, but he had memorized them over dinner. She had eaten no more than a finch would have.

He finished his phone conversation, with some semblance of dignity, he hoped, but remained where he was as Moira meekly allowed her friend to give her a good dressing-down.

Leonard hovered by William's shoulder. "It appears you were right, Your Majesty. She should pose no problems."

"Yes." William reluctantly admitted to himself that he had hoped for a little more backbone. Had he imagined determination in her eyes when she was presented to him? He hoped so; he did not wish for their children to be so amenable.

If this *was* typical behavior on her part, all that he had bargained for would come to him easily now. Her arrival would eventually bring him a larger country and more power, without the hassle of someone to stand up for herself and question his tactics.

When the dog pulled back its lip and snarled at its owner, it was Moira who leaned forward and soothed it with a gentle pat.

She was very unroyal. Very unqueenly. And yet, somehow, very charmingly American.

WHEN THEIR PLANE approached Texas, Chloe, Moira, and Emma drifted toward the three chairs closest to the door, as if some silent beacon drew them there; they couldn't resist. Chloe and Moira had been best friends for ten years, and they were about to separate, never to see each other again. Moira and Emma had been together for sixteen years, the closest thing to family either of them had known in all that time. Even though Chloe knew she was going to be the one in the public eye, she had Emma to help her. Moira was going to be on her own.

By the time they landed in Dallas, Friday, who had been Chloe's "family" for the past three years, was plastered to her knee as if the dog knew something was about to change. Emma's eyes shimmered with emotion, Moira was silent, and Chloe couldn't look at either of them without choking up.

So as the plane taxied toward its destination, she looked at William, which was a very easy thing to do. He'd put on a red tie a little while ago. Now he rose from his chair, stretched up to his full height, buttoned his jacket and stepped toward Chloe.

"You may remain on the plane while I am at my appointment," he offered in a friendly manner, "or, if you prefer, my driver can take you to see any of the sights."

Even as emotional as she was at losing her best friends, Chloe knew that William, broad-shouldered and regal in his power tie and charcoal suit, was the best-looking sight in all of Texas. Put a Resistol and cowboy boots on the man, and there'd be a stampede of women in his direction even before they got a load of his European accent.

"I'll stay on board, thanks."

Emma nudged her, and Chloe knew it should have been "thank you."

*I'll do better.*

"Miss Marshall—" William addressed the Americanized Moira "—it is my understanding that you are staying in Dallas?"

Moira's automatic "Yes" quickly stretched to a nice, drawled-out "Yeah."

"Perhaps you would like to share my limousine? The driver can drop you anywhere after I make my appointment."

"Thank you, Your Majesty."

Chloe and Moira, at the same time, engulfed each other in a spontaneous hug. The dog snarled and barked.

"You really mustn't," Emma whispered in Chloe's ear. "You're a princess now."

"But I'm not," Moira said, and turned and held the woman who'd reared and protected her.

Chloe watched a tear slide down Emma's cheek, which just provoked more tears on Chloe's part, and she caught William's frown at what he probably considered very radical behavior for a royal princess's private secretary.

Chloe, who was losing not one best friend, but two, hugged Friday one last time and held the leash out to Moira. "Take good care of her, okay?"

"Yeah, sure."

"Promise me…Chloe."

Moira took the leash. "I promise." She headed toward the door, which had been opened. The dog planted all four feet and braced herself. Moira tugged one way, Friday the other.

Chloe's heart broke. She turned to Emma, who shook her head. They'd been over this before. Chloe couldn't take the dog with her. She gave Friday a go-ahead wave with her hand, but it didn't do any good.

Moira dragged Friday, growling, toward the door, then stood back and let King William go first. Leonard dashed forward and put himself between William and the dog.

Chloe watched William and Moira walk, and drag, across the well-lit tarmac toward the black limousine. Leonard followed.

"Well, Emma, there she goes."

Emma sniffed.

Chloe squeezed her hand. "She'll be fine."

"I hope so, Your Highness."

"I just hope she doesn't goof up in the limo."

"That will be the easy part."

"Yeah, if she doesn't let the dog bite the king." Chloe watched William duck his head as he folded his body into the limo. "It'd be a shame to damage such a nice pair of—"

"Your Highness!"

Chloe grinned. "Trousers, Emma. I was going to say trousers."

Even though she was noticing not the trousers, but what was in them. And anticipating his return to the jet.

WILLIAM SETTLED HIMSELF into the limousine. He probably should spend the drive thinking about his up-coming meeting with Dr. Lowenstein and how to recruit the man for Baesland, but he had more important things on his mind just then. Information.

"It seems you are very close to Her Royal Highness, Miss Marshall."

"Please, call me Chloe."

The dog growled at her.

"It is too bad your dog is not as fond of you as Her Highness." He noticed Leonard was ready to pounce on the animal, should the need arise.

"Yeah, she kind of took a liking to Moira. Too bad she couldn't have gone home with her."

"You would not miss your dog?" Personally, William had never developed a bond with an animal, but he understood it to be quite common.

"Of course I would. I love my dog."

William was too polite to argue the lack of wisdom in loving an animal that could tear her hand off. Princess Moira, on the other hand, had suffered at the teeth of a dog long ago, and yet apparently liked the animal. Very puzzling.

William chose his words carefully. "Are you meeting someone here in Dallas?"

"No. Why do you ask?"

"You are quite pretty. I thought surely you must have a fiancé or a boyfriend."

Miss Marshall shook her head, apparently off in her own world and not about to make this easy for him.

"I suppose Her Highness is leaving someone behind?" he hinted.

That got her attention, and she answered with a hint of a smile. "Someone?"

"She is very beautiful. I imagine she has broken more than one heart by returning home."

"Just the dog's."

William could not believe his luck. He would not have to wait for her to heal a broken heart. He could spend time with her—they could go riding together in the countryside. They could start as friends. If she could care for a disagreeable dog, maybe she could come to care for him. Maybe even before her father broke the news.

# Chapter Three

Chloe, tucked into the most comfortable bed she'd ever slept in, got a good night's sleep on the jet as it winged toward central Europe. A morning person by nature, she always woke up on her own shortly after dawn. So today, when she rolled over, opened her eyes and saw that it was light out, she hopped right out of bed and headed for the en suite bathroom.

She'd changed and showered in it last night, enjoyed the decadence that money and royal blood provided, and that inspired her off-key stab at "Wouldn't It Be Loverly?' She'd been quite amused with her new lyric, "All I want is a shower in a plane."

She'd thought by this morning she'd be used to it—from the hand-painted ceiling, marble walls, and gold taps, all the way down to the intricately laid floor—but she still marveled over the extravagant expense of one small room. She caught herself improvising, "Lots of gold for me to touch," and promptly shut up before she was overheard.

Someone—since she didn't have a personal maid yet, she knew it had to be Emma—had hung a red silk suit on the bathroom door handle for her, where she was sure not to miss it.

"Oh, Emma," she whispered.

Moira never wore red. This suit was just for Chloe.

All the accessories she needed were laid out on the dresser. She'd seen the gold jewelry before, on Moira, and couldn't believe it was now hers, to wear or not, whatever she decided.

Emma knocked and peeked in. "Good morning, Your Highness. I just wanted to be sure you were awake."

"Emma, come in."

"Yes, Your Highness." Emma stepped into the room and closed the door behind her.

"Thank you for the suit."

"It was nothing, Your Highness."

Chloe smiled softly. "No wonder she adored you so much." She didn't have to say who; they both knew.

"She did?" Emma blushed and grasped the doorknob, as if to escape. "I mean, thank you, Your Highness. We'll be landing soon, so I came to suggest that you take a seat."

"Oh, okay." She thought she should class that up a little, and added, in a more dignified tone, "Thank you, Emma."

"Your Highness." Emma closed the door softly behind her.

Chloe wasted no time; she didn't want to keep anyone waiting on her. She hurried back to the bathroom for one last check of her French braid, which she still wasn't sure she'd gotten symmetrical.

She made only one mistake. It hadn't dawned on her to knock on her own bathroom door until she pulled it open and rushed in to find she was sharing space with William.

And he with no more than a fluffy white towel wrapped around his hips.

"Oh!"

Tall, dark, and handsome in a suit, he was quite stunning out of one.

"Excuse me, Your Majesty."

She should have shut the door before she embarrassed herself further, before she could sweep over his body with an admiring gaze. His hair was damp, his torso bare, his chest broad and smooth. It was quite obvious the broad shoulders she'd noticed yesterday hadn't been enhanced by any padding in his jacket. The only control she could muster at that point was to refuse to let her gaze wander over the towel and beyond.

"Leonard came in a short while ago and told me it is time to take a seat," he said, with a hint of a smile breaking through the dark shadow of morning whiskers.

"Yes, Emma did, too." She wondered how she even came up with such a coherent reply when she should have been backing out the door faster than the plane was flying. "I mean, she came and told me the same thing. In my room," she babbled.

"Are you all right, Your Highness?"

"Hmm? Yes, yes, I'm fine." She pasted on a smile. "Why do you ask?"

Something she probably shouldn't have asked, she noted, as his smile widened and his eyes twinkled.

"No reason." He held out his hand to her.

She stared at it. It was large, strong-looking, tanned. A ruby, set in gold and surrounded by diamonds, adorned his ring finger. It looked very regal and official, not at all like a wedding band. But then, what did she know of royal jewelry? Absolutely nothing. She hoped it wasn't customary to curtsy and kiss his ring or something first thing in the morning. Emma had never mentioned anything like that, but then, Emma hadn't planned on the king at all.

She jumped when William leaned toward her and took her hand in his. When he pulled her toward his room, she dug in her heels.

"All right, then, we will go into your room," he said.

Which meant he stepped right up to her, put his hands on her shoulders and spun her around toward the door through which she had come. She walked forward—she really had no choice with him guiding her like that—and, before she knew it, she was sitting in an upholstered chair, knee-to-knee with him in an adjacent one.

His towel slid upward as he sat, then gapped open over one thigh, revealing sturdy muscle and more tanned flesh than her shaky composure could handle at the moment.

"Oh, there you are, Your Majesty," Leonard said tonelessly as he passed through the bathroom and into Chloe's room. He stood very erect, his arms parallel to his body. "Will you be needing anything else?"

"Not until we land."

With William's eyes no longer on her, Chloe let her gaze drift lower, beyond the towel's edge, over his knees, down to his bare feet and back up again. She'd never admired a man's legs before. Heck, she'd never admired any part of a king before, but she was ogling most all of one now.

He seemed perfectly comfortable with his near nakedness. Did he parade around in front of his queen this way? Did he have a queen?

"Find yourself a seat somewhere," he told Leonard.

"Yes, Your Majesty."

She snapped her eyes back up into decent territory, only to find she was too late. His grin said he knew perfectly well where she'd been.

The plane bumped down and started to taxi.

"There, now I can shave." William rose, headed for the bathroom, but then turned back to Chloe. "Is there anything you need in here first? I can wait." He held out his arm in an invitation for her to brush past him.

She bolted to her feet. "No. Thank you." She glanced around the room as she searched for the nearest exit. "I'm going to go...out now."

Just when she was almost to the correct door and into safer territory, he spoke again. "Your brother said he was sorry he cannot be at the airport to meet you."

"Mmm, okay." She pulled the door open without looking back.

"And Leonard informs me that the airport is packed with people from Ennsway waiting to see you after so many years."

*Packed?*

She hesitated on the threshold to see if there was a punch line to this news. Although what could be worse? She wanted to dip her toe into this princess role and get used to it slowly, and it seemed she was about to be get a quick dunking.

She needed questions answered, like was the king married? She needed tutoring, as in how to greet a crowd of people at the airport. She needed Emma right behind her, whispering instructions in her ear, all the way to the castle.

And she'd thought she was in over her head when she saw William in nothing more than a towel.

WILLIAM LEANED over the vanity and peered into the mirror, pulling his face this way and that as the electric razor buzzed his whiskers away. He preferred a blade, but not when flying, for obvious reasons. If an occasional air pocket did not cause nicks, then the way Princess Moira had looked at him would have.

She was supposed to be a virgin. King Albert, her father, had practically guaranteed it.

A virgin would be shy around a half-naked man.

His hand jerked, and the razor pinched the skin beneath his nose. "Ow."

Leonard's face appeared in the wide mirror beside his. "Is everything all right, Your Majesty?"

"Fine, Leonard."

He was less than half-naked, he was barely covered.

A virgin would have blushed and turned her eyes away.

"Ow. Damn!"

Leonard's face gave nothing away. "Trouble, Your Majesty?"

William set the razor on the marble with a thud. A good, solid thud to get his mind off the princess's experience with men—or lack thereof—and onto delivering her to her father before his afternoon nap. "This blasted thing is dull."

"Sure it is," Leonard mumbled.

"Speak up, man."

"I said I will see that it is taken care of today. Perhaps Your Majesty is unhappy with Her Highness?"

William combed his already combed hair and brushed past his secretary. As usual, his suit had been laid out by his valet, and all William had to do was get dressed. He did not even have the luxury of another task to take his mind off Princess Moira.

Leonard continued, "I could call King Albert's secretary and see if the old man is having second thoughts."

"That will not be necessary." As a matter of fact, William was having second thoughts of his own. They had to do with the heat he had seen in Moira's eyes. Perhaps she was not so meek after all. Perhaps instead of him educating a shy virgin on their wedding night, they would both enjoy a more passionate encounter. Perhaps...ahead of schedule.

"I just thought if Your Majesty is displeased with the princess, and if her father is willing to void the contract—"

"Over my dead body!"

Leonard's cheek twitched as he restrained a smile. "As you wish, Your Majesty."

William seldom rushed to or for anything; he was a king, and his world waited on him. But today he dressed quickly and rushed to the lounge, and he knew it was because he was in a hurry to see Moira again. To see if she still had heat in her eyes or if she would successfully mask it. To see if she still looked as stunning in red silk as she had earlier or if the soft look about her was due to just waking up. To see if he was as distracted in her presence as he had been in the past fifteen minutes without her.

IF THE AIRPORT in Santa Barbara was small, the one in Baesland was downright minuscule, a speck on a map at most, a dot on the side of a green mountain. The terminal had only one gate and no other planes in sight. There were, however, scores of people crowded near the entrance to the building.

After the door of King William's jet opened, Chloe

waited just inside, eager to see her new home, anxious about proper etiquette. Sunlight streamed in and bathed her in its heat. Children shouted, "There she is!" and "I saw her!"

Emma hovered just behind Chloe's shoulder, a little to one side, and quietly offered advice. "You may wave if you like, Your Highness, but wait here for His Majesty. You'll follow him down the steps."

"Okay." Chloe tested a small wave and got cheers in response.

The crowd on the tarmac below swelled to hundreds of men and women, old and young, and children.

"Shouldn't they be in school?"

"This is a historic occasion for them, Your Highness. They were given a holiday to come greet you."

They held signs reading Welcome Home HRH and We Love You, Princess Moira. They waved banners and small Ennsway flags with their distinctive red, gold, and green diagonal stripes.

"I was told they've been here since before noon."

"Noon?" Chloe glanced at her wrist to check her watch, but she'd handed it over to Moira with the rest of her possessions. It seemed a princess didn't need a watch. "I thought it was morning."

"It is midafternoon," William replied.

As she heard his deep voice, Chloe turned and watched him stroll through the lounge toward her. She was much happier to see him fully dressed in dark pants and a jacket, his white shirt collar open at the neck, than to see him in a towel. He looked no less manly, and her heart still skipped two beats when she recalled his smooth chest.

"Though it probably feels like morning to you, due

to the time difference.'' William glanced out the door to the tarmac below. "My, look at all the people.''

Chloe and Emma had had a few minutes to chat before his appearance. According to Emma, William was a bachelor king, with no announcements of a queen anticipated in the near future. "Though one never knows about the negotiations that go on behind closed doors,'' Emma had added.

Chloe took note of William's height, his dark good looks, the self-assurance he exuded just standing there, and imagined that every princess in the world hoped for such negotiations on their behalf.

"Shall we?'' William asked.

Chloe, puzzled as to why he was asking her instead of stepping forward as Emma had said he would, nodded her agreement.

He extended his arm toward the stairs, definitely indicating that she should go first.

She hesitated.

"You have nothing to fear,'' he offered quietly. "Your people love you.''

"Your people'' had a nice ring to it, but that wasn't the part bothering her.

"And I will be right behind you.''

*That* was. Behind her back, she latched on to Emma's hand. "Oh, no, I couldn't, Your Majesty. You go first.''

*And I'll keep Emma right behind me.*

"But I insist, Your Highness. Your people would never forgive me for stealing this moment from them.''

Emma nudged Chloe gently in the back, and she deduced that she really had no choice without looking fearful or childish, neither of which appealed to her.

"Well, thank you, Your Majesty. That's mighty nice of you." Another nudge. "I mean, how thoughtful."

Chloe thought she could feel Emma rolling her eyes behind her, but, of course, that wasn't possible. Emma never rolled her eyes.

Chloe stepped through the doorway onto the portable landing. Should she pause and wave? Should she descend immediately, so as not to hold up the king? *What would a real princess do?*

In the end, she paused briefly and waved a genuine, friendly, American wave. It seemed to be the right thing to do, as the crowd cheered and waved back.

"Are these people all from Ennsway?" she asked Emma over her shoulder.

Only it wasn't Emma who was there.

"Some are from Baesland," William murmured above her ear. "My people also have anticipated your return."

*What would Moira say if she were here?*

It wouldn't be so hard to figure out, if William wasn't standing so close, if his arm didn't brush against her shoulder, and if he didn't smell so darned good from whatever herbal shampoo was available in this part of the world.

"How nice." It sounded stilted and phony to her, but seemed to go over well with William.

WILLIAM DID NOT LISTEN to what Princess Moira said so much as he watched her body language. The way she reached for her secretary from time to time, at the door of the plane, at the bottom of the steps, then again as she approached the Mercedes limousine, showed that the princess clearly relied too much on Emma. It was not good for anyone to have so much influence over a member of the royal family.

"Sit by the window so everyone can see you," Emma said, and the princess did so.

The driver left the airstrip slowly, due to all the people. They surrounded the limousine and walked beside it, all smiles and waves. The princess waved and smiled back. William lowered his window, and noticed that the princess glanced at her secretary before she lowered hers also.

"You do not mind the wind?" William asked.

She smiled, as if she knew a secret. "No, not at all."

And, as hundreds of people lined up to see her, she continued to smile, in spite of the delay.

Outside the airport, the driver slowed to a snail's pace and announced, "I do not think we will make it to the castle by three o'clock, Your Majesty."

William resigned himself to that fact.

"What's at three o'clock?"

"Your father naps daily at three. He had hoped to see you beforehand."

The princess continued to touch every hand that made it through the window, large or small, clean or questionable. "And we won't make it in time?"

"No, Your Highness."

Parents crowded close to the car and held their children up so that they could see, or be seen, better. They chattered in Ennswayan, their native language. The driver slowed even more and muttered, "Crazy people, they'll get their toes flattened for sure."

"Then perhaps I could get out and meet some of them," she suggested.

William thought it would be quite rude if he showed

how truly surprised he was at her suggestion. "As you wish, Your Highness. Driver, stop the car."

Her secretary opened the door and preceded the princess out onto the road. William got out on his own side. He was a very hands-on king, no stranger or figurehead to his subjects. They approached him as always, with pleasant greetings in either English or Baeslese, and an outstretched hand.

Knowing her father and brother as he did, William had not expected such warmth from the princess. She did not stare at the patches on their pants and jackets. Neither did she shy away as they pressed closer.

A small, round woman, with a tattered blue scarf tied over her hair, grasped Moira's hand and spoke profusely and at great length.

The princess smiled at the woman and said, "Thank you. I'm happy to be home." She repeated it over and over as she walked along the paved road, the limo keeping pace with her.

Some people grasped her hand and, when they heard her speak English, said, "Welcome, Your Highness."

A child held out her arms for a hug, and the princess crouched down—it looked to be a tricky maneuver in her snug skirt and high heels, which were not designed for walking, much less crouching—opened her arms and obliged. After that, every child wanted a hug, and the parents melted back and smiled proudly.

William was pleased.

From time to time, the princess glanced at the mountain beyond, or at the flowers that grew in abundance in front of every shop, and William thought she took it all in as if she were a stranger to this land. A tourist. He tried to imagine what it would be like to return after being gone over half his life. Sixteen years ago, he had been eighteen and had taken an interest in the kingdom that would eventually be his. But at twelve, the age when Moira left, he had been more interested in falconing than progress and ribbon-cutting ceremonies.

A young girl, about four years old, approached with tears on her cheeks and muddy pawprints on her gold sweater and pants. She sniffled and looked uncertain whether to cry or to speak to Her Highness.

The princess held out her arms to her.

The child, with curly red hair and green eyes, hugged the princess, then quickly stepped back and pinned her with an earnest gaze.

"What is it, sweetie?"

"You won't send my puppy away, will you?" the child asked in her own language, which William understood clearly.

The princess brushed the child's cheek dry with her own thumb while she listened to whatever Emma whispered in her ear. "Of course I won't. And you won't cry about it anymore, okay?"

Emma translated to the child, whose eyes lit up.

"You must have a very special puppy. Will you bring him to visit me sometime?"

The child's mouth dropped open in surprise. She was the perfect mirror image of her mother standing behind her. She nodded vigorously.

"Good. Then I'll expect you."

And William's heart warmed as the princess stood up, shook the mother's hand and continued to move along the road. She was quite different from her brother. In a good way, even if she had become uncomfortable with the language of her people and allowed Emma to speak for her. Perhaps, William dared to hope, she would be of advantage to him in ways other than the size of her kingdom.

He would invite her riding later. It was an activity she'd always loved. As he'd hoped, they could begin their partnership with an easy friendship.

CHLOE BIT HER TONGUE for the rest of the drive to Castle Ennsway, the stone curtain wall of which she could see from miles away. The limousine passed through the double-towered gatehouse and outer bailey, then the inner gatehouse, and finally crossed the inner courtyard and stopped in front of a magnificent red-brick great hall.

Chloe had seen Moira's photographs of the castle; they didn't do it justice. Colorful banners of red, gold, and green flew from every tower and flapped in the breeze. They hadn't been in the photos, and Chloe knew they heralded her arrival as a special occasion.

Still, Chloe was miffed.

"Gee, thanks a lot, Emma," she whispered sarcastically as she stepped out of the limousine in front of Castle Ennsway.

"What, Your Highness?"

"Don't play dumb with me." Her gaze strayed around the courtyard, over the lawn, took in the fountain and the colorful gardens. "I knew I needed language lessons."

"There wasn't time. Smile, Your Highness," Emma said through her own pleasant expression.

Chloe ditched the frown and smiled. When she was faced with this beautiful castle she was fixin' to live in, it really wasn't all that difficult.

"It would have been too risky for you to attempt,"

Emma continued. "It's better for you to stick to English than make a mistake.

"Hmph!" Fortunately, none of the people had backed off when she answered them in English, but had smiled and welcomed her in their own stilted attempts at the language. She hadn't understood a word they said otherwise, and they'd seemed pleased by her generic replies of "Thank you" and "I'm so happy to be home."

The castle itself was incredible, not because it was built spectacularly—Chloe wouldn't have known normal from outstanding castle architecture—but because she, personally, had never seen a castle before. It rose before her, several stories tall, with towers and arrow loops, battlements and wallwalks. She'd have thought it was all a dream, but the snap of the banners in the breeze was a sound she couldn't have imagined without actually hearing it herself.

"After you, Your Highness," Emma said, indicating the arched doorway through which Chloe should enter.

The crowd was gone, not permitted past the outer gatehouse. There were servants, however, and they, too, greeted her with broad smiles, bows, and curtsies. Chloe couldn't see any reason to treat them differently from those who had lined the road and, one by one, she shook hands with each.

Inside, Emma whispered, "Straight down this hall."

But Chloe, staring at the walls around her, barely listened. She'd had classes in art, and she knew good work when she saw it. Painstaking murals were painted on the high-ceilinged walls, with delicate friezes carved above. Handwoven tapestries depicted the kingly pursuits of hunting deer, battling invaders and debauchery, with overflowing feasts and equally overflowing women.

"Try not to look like a tourist, Your Highness," Emma whispered in her ear.

"Oh." Chloe reigned in her appreciation for all Moira had grown up with, but which must appear mundane to her now. Later, when she could get some time alone and unobserved, she'd come back to the great hall and study every piece until she could see them all in her sleep. "Right."

"Straight to the other end of the hall, then right and up the stairs. I'll direct you to your father's chamber when we get up there."

"Gotcha. Hey, Emma."

Emma's long-suffering sigh spoke volumes. "Yes, Your Highness?"

Chloe was momentarily speechless as she discovered impressive artwork also lined every passageway through which she walked. Mycenaean vases and Greek busts adorned nooks along walls which were sometimes stone, other times plaster. A jackal-headed Canopic jar, which Chloe fervently hoped did not contain the traditional remains of the dead, occupied its own cranny.

"Do you think it'd be possible for me to stop in a bathroom first?"

Emma grinned—a welcome sight to Chloe in such foreign surroundings. "Of course, Your Highness."

"Good," she said with her own smile of relief. "I wasn't sure what was appropriate when the king might be waiting."

"You're a royal princess, Your Highness. You may do whatever you wish."

Chloe noted that William and Leonard were far

enough behind them not to overhear. They appeared lost in their own conversation.

"I'm sure you'd like to think so, Emma, but I distinctly remember reaching for the door handle in the limo and having you swat my hand away."

"I didn't swat, I brushed."

"Swatted."

Emma didn't retort, but instead said, "Perhaps Your Highness would like a signal from time to time? Up these stairs."

The stone stairs were worn uneven from generations of feet. Chloe resisted the impulse to get down on her knees and run her hand over them, as if she could absorb centuries of history by doing so.

"I think that'd be a dandy idea."

Emma groaned. "Really, Your Highness, the colloquialism you picked up in the States is most unattractive."

"The signal, Emma."

"I don't know. I've never needed one." When Chloe reached the top of the stairs, Emma directed, "Around to your left now."

"Don't let me leave alone. After all these turns, I'll never be able to find my way back."

"I shan't leave your side. Third door on the left is a powder room."

The "powder room" was big enough to party in; so large, in fact, that Chloe felt downright exposed. Toilets were supposed to have walls near them, at least within reaching distance. She was so uncomfortable that she made quick use of the facilities and rushed back out into the hall.

Emma waited alone. "His Majesty has gone ahead to see if your father is awake."

"Good, then we can get our signals down pat." She headed in the direction Emma indicated with a nod. "It should be something natural, so no one will suspect."

"Yes, of course. Should I cough?"

"No, you'll draw attention to yourself."

"Very right, Your Highness. I could wink."

"They'll think you've got a tic. How about if you pat your hair?"

"They'll think I'm vain."

"Hopefully I'll catch on before that happens."

Emma patted her hair. "Is that yes or no?"

"Yes."

"And what about no?"

"Hmm." Chloe got distracted by a particularly elegant gold wall sconce. "Play with your necklace."

"I don't wear jewelry, Your Highness. Up these stairs."

"It's a good thing I'm in great shape from hiking around the campus."

"Instead of the necklace?" Emma reminded her to stay on track.

Chloe really wanted to enjoy her new surroundings, not make up games. She decided to give her royal privileges a test run. "Start wearing one."

"Yes, Your Highness."

*Boy, that was easy.*

"In the meantime, I'll touch the neck of my blouse if I think you're about to blunder." In a matter of minutes, Emma indicated an open doorway, through which voices floated out into the hall. "Do you remember what to do? What to say?"

Chloe took a deep breath and let it out slowly. "Yes."

*I hope.*

Emma patted her hair and said, "Yes," then fingered her neckline and said, "No."

"Gotcha."

Emma sighed audibly.

"Don't worry. It's just the two of us."

"It's most imperative, Your Highness, not to ever think it's just the two of us."

Chloe stepped into the king's bedchamber and struggled to keep her mouth from gaping open at the pure luxury of it. It was so large—larger than her entire apartment in Santa Barbara—and so rich with hunter green silk draping the windows, covering the walls and swathing the bedposts, that it made the king—her *father*—appear quite small and pale. White-haired and gaunt, he reclined in his bed, his back and shoulders propped up by a mound of velvet pillows, royal purple with golden tassels at each corner.

"Father," she said. She crossed the room quickly to his bedside and held out her hands.

He wheezed and coughed for a moment, then took her hands in his cold grasp. "Moira...you have grown into a lovely woman. You—" Another cough and wheeze. "You look like your mother when she was your age." His pale face lit up in a smile.

"Father, I had no idea you were so ill."

King Albert waved away her distress.

"You could have come sooner," sniped a voice from the corner.

Chloe turned and saw a lean, bearded man. He looked so much like Moira, she had no doubt this was her brother, Prince Louis. The one who was supposed to spend so much time out of the country and cause her no trouble.

"Then you would have seen for yourself how much you were needed here," Louis said.

"Hello, Louis." How old had he been when Moira had left? Ten? "You've grown quite tall."

He stepped forward, looking at her closely as he advanced. "I had given up on requesting your presence for Father."

Chloe didn't know what to say. Neither Moira nor Emma had mentioned more than the recent request that had prompted their switch. Had Moira lied by omission? Or had someone not told Moira that she was needed here?

"I must nap now, Moira," King Albert said. "But first, I have good news." He wheezed, caught his breath and glanced at William. "Perhaps I shall wait until later. You must be tired from your journey."

"His Majesty took good care of me."

"Yes, I knew he would." He coughed again. "Let me rest now."

"Yes, Father."

"We will talk soon."

Chloe patted the old man's hand. His skin was thin and dry as paper. His eyes drifted closed, and he looked at peace.

Her brother, however, tossed her a hostile glare that made her want to crawl under the bed.

# *Chapter Four*

"Emma," Chloe said softly as they adjourned to the passageway outside her father's bedroom, "I need a tour of the castle ASAP. The room 'I' had as a child, my favorite places, that sort of thing."

"Yes, Your Highness, I was thinking the very same thing."

She tried to wiggle her toes to uncramp them and remembered why she preferred her old boots. "Right after I get out of these heels. How did she wear them for hours at a time?"

"*She* did not walk alongside limousines." Even with Emma's dry tone, it sounded like a compliment. "Now, bid King William goodbye, and we will begin."

Chloe turned toward the three men exiting her father's suite. She pointedly ignored her brother's glare and concentrated instead on a very relieved-looking William. "Your Majesty—"

"Your father looks better today," he said positively. "I think he is quite pleased to have you home again."

She'd thought King Albert looked like death warmed over.

William's smile was warm and genuine, his gaze smoldering. "But not as pleased as I am," he added.

No man had ever looked at Chloe quite that way before, and it took her a moment to compose her speech. "Thank you, Your Majesty. And thank you, also, for the use of your plane. It made the trip home quite pleasant."

*There, that wasn't so bad. I'll just pretend I'm in a play, and, before long, it'll be second nature to talk so darned tactfully all the time. So prissy and highfalutin.*

"Your Highness, would you like to go riding?"

She looked at William closely, to see whether he was extending the invitation out of duty, but he actually looked eager.

"I was fixin' to—" She took a deep breath and tried again. "I thought I'd go to my room for a while."

"But, Your Highness, you have too much energy to be tired. Surely you do not intend to spend your first day home closed up inside."

Out of the corner of her eye, Chloe caught Emma patting her hair. Chloe was free to go, except for one thing. She didn't even know how to get out of the castle to get to the stables—a fact that served to emphasize that one-on-one time with Emma was an absolute necessity.

"It's very kind of you, Your Majesty. Perhaps I could have a rain check?"

"Rain check?" William's brows puckered ever so slightly, an amusing sight above his lopsided grin. "Ah, that must be one of your American expressions."

"Oh, I'm sorry. I mean, would it be all right if I took you up on your offer at a later date?"

"Tomorrow, perhaps."

She was glad to see that she hadn't hurt his feelings. Who could say what a king thought when he got turned down? A king probably never got put off. Especially not William, not with those gold flecks in his eyes twinkling the way they were now. If she didn't have groundwork to cover...

"Maybe I'll see you then. And thanks...thank you again." Chloe turned toward Emma, caught a barely perceptible nod indicating which direction to go, and headed that way.

She hadn't gone more than a step when William said, "Your Highness—"

She pivoted back toward him before she remembered she was wearing high heels, not sturdy cowboy boots, on a marble floor. She bobbled. He shot out a hand in reflex, but she regained her balance just as he grasped her elbow.

"Are you all right?" he asked.

"Yeah, just these darned—"

His eyebrows shot up.

"Uh, yes, I'm fine. Thank you for being so quick."

"My pleasure," he said, with just the slightest little bow of his head, which only served to draw her attention to the warmth in his eyes.

"Uh, you can let go of my elbow now."

He released her slowly, letting his fingers slide off her sleeve. "Your American accent is quite enchanting, Your Highness."

All the same, Chloe didn't want to give up the game just yet. "It is? Oh, well, thank you. All those years in America, I was bound to pick one up."

"Would you join me for dinner this evening?"

_Persistent devil._

Again Emma, who had her back to them and was pretending to be deeply engrossed in a painting on the wall and not paying them any attention, patted her hair.

"That's very nice of you. I'd like that, of course,

but it's my first day home, and I should dine with my father.''

"Well, I shall have to settle for riding tomorrow, then. Say ten o'clock?''

Chloe loved morning rides, and she should know her way around the castle well enough by then. She smiled in anticipation, both of riding and of seeing him again. They could venture out together across the countryside, just the two of them. The breeze in her face, dew on the grass, a good horse beneath her, a handsome king beside her—what more could a former Texas cowgirl ask for?

William gently grasped her arms as he had when they met on the plane, dipped his head and closed the gap between them. Mesmerized by his lapis eyes, straight nose and firm chin coming closer and closer, Chloe found herself staring until she was cross-eyed. His cheek was warm on hers, and his lips were firm as he graced both cheeks with the same silken treatment.

And, if she was not mistaken, he lingered while he was at it, too. Although she might have felt that way simply because, when his head dipped, her heart lurched into her throat and remained there.

"Until tomorrow," he whispered in her ear.

He turned and left. She couldn't move. She was grateful that Leonard accompanied him and Louis disappeared, leaving her alone with Emma.

"Your Highness."

Chloe sighed, letting her breath out slowly, melting a little as she watched him walk down the hall with a long, purposeful stride and start down the steps. The last thing she saw was the top of his head, his dark hair thick and luscious and begging her to dream about him tonight.

As HE WALKED OUT of the great hall and down the stone steps, William had a sudden, inexplicable craving for chocolate. It took him a moment to realize he was also quietly humming a catchy tune about the same. The very same tune he had heard Moira singing on his jet. He glanced at Leonard to see whether he had overheard, but one could seldom read the secretary's expression.

Unlike Princess Moira, whose bright eyes and open smile hid nothing. Noting her pleasure at being home again and seeing her castle after such a long absence was like watching a child's face light up at Christmas. Her concern for her father's health was admirable. And her warm anticipation of his kiss—that was not to be forgotten. She had tensed up when he had kissed her on the plane, as if she had not expected it. She had been more relaxed this time, more supple in his grasp, less resistant.

As a man, he thought she rather liked his kisses. Maybe even read more into them than a traditional greeting. But he wanted to be her friend—and soon, before she learned of the marriage contract. All he could do was hope her father did not break the news over dinner tonight. If not, he could start on his friendship campaign at ten o'clock tomorrow morning.

CHLOE FOLLOWED EMMA for what seemed like thirty minutes—down halls, up stairs, along corridors—before Emma finally stopped, opened a wooden door recessed in a deep archway and stood back to let Chloe enter first.

Instead, Chloe balanced herself with one hand on the plaster wall and removed her heels with the other. "I need a foot massage. And a map."

Emma grinned. "It *is* rather large by American standards."

Chloe snickered. "UCSB could hold classes in here. How many rooms are there?"

"One hundred thirty."

*And I thought I'd be able to find my way out in the morning?*

"More or less."

"You've lost some rooms?" she teased.

"It depends on which ones you want to count. Is the dungeon considered one room, or three?"

"I see."

Emma extended her arm to indicate that Chloe should enter first. "This is your suite, Your Highness."

When Chloe's mouth dropped open in shock, she knew she'd done the right thing in turning down William's offer. She really had to acclimate herself to all this wealth before she gave herself away. "This is my bedroom?"

"This is your sitting room. You may dine here if you like. Do needlework—" Emma looked at Chloe, whom she'd known for years, and amended, "Yes, well, watch television, perhaps."

Chloe listened to her, of course, but walked around the suite, touching Roman busts and vases that should have been in a museum. On second thought, she quit touching. "This stuff is priceless."

Emma smiled indulgently. "His Majesty thinks your American speech is, too, Your Highness. Perhaps you should not try so hard to speak...properly, after all."

Chloe didn't even pretend to be insulted. "Deal!"

Emma scratched her head. "Yes, that's precisely what I mean."

"But won't that make people suspicious?"

"There is nothing to be suspicious of, Your Highness, so you might as well be genuine. You've been gone so many years, I think they expect to see something exotic and foreign come home. I expect my own speech has undergone some changes." She said it as though she wasn't proud of it.

Chloe pointed at a set of gilt-bordered, cream-colored double doors. "What's in there?"

"This is all your suite. Have at it."

It was Chloe's turn to grin indulgently at Emma. "Yeah, I'd say you'd picked up a little slang, too."

She pushed open the doors and found a bed canopied and draped with creamy lace, enough antique furniture to put a warehouse in business, and a hardwood floor mostly covered with plush, handwoven rugs. Off that room was a bathroom with a sunken tub surrounded by marble pillars and a small forest.

"I'm almost afraid to see the closet." It was probably as large as her old apartment.

"Your maid will get you whatever you want or need."

"Aw, c'mon, Emma, don't spoil the fun."

"Very well. Just around this corner."

It was large, but not *that* large. More like Chloe's old living room. A maid in her early twenties, wearing a gray dress and white apron, blushed, dipped into a quick curtsy, then continued hanging up Moira's clothes—the ones that would fit Chloe—and new ones that Emma had picked out in the past week just for Chloe. Rack upon rack of new shoes in every imaginable color filled one wall.

"This is Angela, Your Highness. She will be your personal maid."

Chloe smiled warmly, eager to get off to a good start with people she'd see every day. "Hello, Angela."

"Your Highness." Angela gestured toward the red high-heeled shoes dangling from Chloe's hand and asked in halting English, "You would like for me to take the shoes?"

Chloe felt ridiculous handing someone else her shoes to put away, but she did it. She was a princess and was expected to act as such. "Angela, when you come across them, could you bring me my DKNY jeans and UCSB sweatshirt?"

She'd just given her first order to her maid. *Her maid!* If that wasn't a hoot, nothing was.

Angela's brows puckered. "DK...Your Highness?"

"DKNY."

Still puckered.

"Angela can't read, Your Highness," Emma said very matter-of-factly.

Chloe's glance darted over to Emma and back to Angela. "Oh."

"You thought I could read?" Angela asked in surprise.

"Well—"

Chloe left just enough space for Emma to jump in.

"The educational system hasn't changed much since you left, Your Highness," Emma interjected. "Ennsway has very few readers. Just look for the new jeans and a navy sweatshirt, Angela. Now, if Your Highness would like to follow me..."

Chloe took the hint, slipped into a pair of sneakers and followed Emma on a tour of the castle. She saw the cozy nursery where Moira had begun her life. The gymnasium-size playroom she'd shared with her brother, Louis, with shelves that still overflowed with dolls, storybooks, and toys of all sizes and shapes. Her mother's chambers, which Moira had visited frequently until she was ten and her mother had died. The general direction of Louis's room, though there was no need to venture there. The dining room with murals, inset panels, and a highly polished trestle table long enough to feed an army. The general location of the kitchen, another place Emma assured Chloe she wouldn't have need to visit.

"What if I get hungry in the middle of the night?" Chloe asked as they walked side by side along another stone passageway.

"Then you ring your maid."

"What if all I want is a pop-up?"

"There are no pop-ups in the castle."

"No pop-ups? That does it. Send someone to the store immediately," she teased.

"Impossible."

"But you said I'm a princess and can do whatever I want."

"That is absolutely correct, but there are no pop-ups in Ennsway."

Chloe couldn't imagine such a thing. "Why not?"

"We import very little."

"Can that be changed?"

"Of course."

"Good," she said cheerfully. "Import some. Strawberry is my favorite. Now what?"

"I thought you might enjoy this room." Emma stepped aside and let Chloe enter the library. "I know how you love to study a variety of subjects. Many of these volumes are in English."

Books lined the dark wood shelves from floor to ceiling. To the right, a carved wood balustrade followed stairs up to a second story and along the edge of the loft. Each wall had a ladder that slid along brass guides so that every book was accessible by anyone interested. Architecture, art, fairy tales, history…to zoology.

"I thought people here couldn't read."

"They can't. Members of the royal family are well educated, however."

"Sounds positively archaic."

"Welcome home, Your Highness. Now, if you'd like to return to your suite, your masseuse should be ready."

"My masseuse? Really?"

"Yes, Your Highness. You indicated you would like a foot massage, I believe?"

She hadn't meant it *literally*. She was used to making wishes that were never granted. If they were all going to start coming true now, she wondered what she should wish about William.

TEN O'CLOCK came way too early the next morning for Chloe. Normally up with the sun and in bed at a reasonable hour each evening, she was now hours off schedule thanks to jet lag. To her, it felt like eleven at night.

She could turn this to her advantage. If she made a mistake, she'd blame it on being half-asleep.

It wasn't only the time change that had kept her awake last night, though. It was also knowing she'd see William this morning. It was hoping he'd kiss her again. It was debating whether she could turn her head at just the right moment, capture his lips—and get away with it.

As those thoughts raced through her mind, a servant moved silently in her sitting room. He set the small table with delicate china, highly polished silver, sparkling crystal, and fresh flowers. When he was finished, every piece that bore a monogram was turned in exactly the same direction. Her napkin was folded at a precise angle to the place setting. He stepped back, chewed his lip as he scrutinized the table for any imperfections, then noticed Chloe and bowed.

He nearly tripped over his feet to hold her chair before she could get settled in by herself, then proceeded to uncover steaming dishes. In stilted English, he offered her a selection of pastries, eggs cooked three different ways, and several meats—though she couldn't have said for sure just what kind.

And then he disappeared and left Chloe alone to enjoy her breakfast. It was just as well. She really only wanted her customary pop-ups, but she was afraid she'd hurt someone's feelings if she didn't at least sample a little of everything.

She was eager to see William again. She rushed through her taste test—difficult to do when it was all delicious—then summoned Emma, whom she needed for directions to the stables.

Chloe, in the jeans she preferred, and Emma, in a dress suitable for following Her Highness all day, walked outside together. Chloe had always thought Rancho Santa Ynez to be top-notch. If so, then Castle Ennsway horses must be in heaven. The long brick building had private paddocks for each stall on the far side and, on the near, half doors beneath a wide roof so that each horse could hang its head out and seek attention from any one of the abundance of grooms hired to tend them.

She spotted William right away and remembered the fantasies she'd enjoyed.

He immediately left the half-dozen men with whom he'd been conversing and strode over to her. "Your Highness." If his smile was any indication, he was as happy to see her as she was him.

"Your Majesty." She burned to toss formality aside and test his name on her lips, but couldn't do so in front of everyone. They'd be off together soon now. Alone.

"Good morning." William stepped closer and reached for her.

She leaned into his grasp, waited breathlessly for his kisses and decided formality had its good points. Except his touch was too brief today, doubtless because of their audience.

"I have a present for you," he said proudly. At a snap of his fingers, a flashy gray Andalusian mount was led forward, head high, ears forward, large brown eyes curious. "I know she looks like a handful, but, I assure you, she is as sweet as candy. Not that you would be unable to handle her, of course."

*Why, he's babbling. As nervous as any man with an expensive gift for a woman he barely knows.*

"She's beautiful, Your Majesty."

*Too expensive, unfortunately.*

Now, how did one turn down a gift from a king? Especially one she wanted. The horse, not the king.

*Well, him, too.*

"I can't believe you would do this for me." She was thinking on her feet and not very well on so little sleep. "I mean—"

His smile wavered. His brows puckered until he had a little crease between them.

"It's too generous—"

Emma moved into Chloe's line of vision, patting her

hair as if they'd just come through a windstorm. Did that mean "Yes" as in "It's okay to accept it," or "Yes" as in "It's good to reject it"? Emma's horrified expression provided the answer.

"Well, I just don't know what to say," Chloe finished lamely, and then added a brilliant smile.

William's frown quickly changed back to his lopsided grin. "I am sorry. My English is not as good as I thought, apparently. Do you like her?"

Chloe took the reins from the groom's hand and patted the mare's neck. "Yes. In fact, I think I may be in love."

"With the mare? I would have to be American to understand?"

"No, you'd have to be female." She wanted to erase any confusion he might have. "She's beautiful. Thank you, Your Majesty. I'm really…"

She laughed at the sheer joy of trying to find the right words, since she couldn't just throw caution to the wind and her arms around his neck.

"…overwhelmed."

"Shall we try her out, then?"

"Yes."

A groomsman stepped forward to give Chloe a leg up, something she wouldn't have minded since the mare was tacked with an English saddle. But William brushed the man aside, bent at the waist and held his hands out, waiting for Chloe to flex her knee so that he could lace his fingers beneath it and boost her up.

She did so with pleasure, and darned near tumbled over the mare's back.

William's hand landed on her thigh to steady her, but did nothing of the kind. "Your Highness?"

"I'm fine, thank you."

"You are sure?"

It was a good thing she'd never met an American man with so much gentlemanly concern, or she might have been married by now and unable to take advantage of this opportunity. She shuddered at the thought.

"You would like a different mount, perhaps?"

"No way."

He lingered near her leg.

"Better mount up, Your Majesty, or you'll get left behind."

Relief washed over his face then, and he quickly seated himself on his own jet-black mount.

Chloe and Moira had had many friendly bets over the years, and usually they wagered that the loser had to switch to English or Western, whichever the case may be. Moira had run a few hundred barrels—she refused to try any trick riding, regardless of the wager—and Chloe had learned to jump without getting left behind. So she wasn't entirely at a loss with a slippery saddle, no horn, and plow reining. Just a little.

"Where are we going this morning?" she asked, impatient to be alone with him.

William looked as eager as she felt. "I thought you might like to ride to the river."

"Sounds wonderful. Lead the way."

"Mount up," William said to a half-dozen men.

Chloe felt her breezy mood slip a notch. "They're coming with us?"

"Of course, Your Highness. You did not ride with an escort in the United States?"

That was an understatement. A couple of cowboys here and there in Texas, and they hadn't been escorts so much as ardent pursuers. "No."

William glared at Emma. "That should never have been allowed."

Chloe felt bad for putting Emma in such a position. "I insisted, Your Majesty. It was perfectly safe there, and I needed the time alone."

"It is safe here, but I must insist."

He said it in such a way that it could only be taken as genuine concern. She took a deep breath, pasted on a smile and willingly gave in. As a princess, she supposed, she could have stormed off until she got her way, but then she'd have missed riding with William.

They warmed up the horses for a mile, let them out for a frisky lope after that and then settled into a companionable trot, side by side. Their escorts followed at a discreet distance, so they were almost alone. Enough to talk freely. Chloe was dying to call him "William" instead of "Your Majesty."

He nodded toward a steep hill ahead and to the right. "That would be a good location for a health care facility, Your Highness."

"Yes," she said, feigning interest. "Please, call me Moira."

She was rewarded with a warm smile that lit up his eyes.

"If you will call me William."

"I'd like that...William." It felt so good to finally say it, she almost got giddy.

"You blush beautifully, Moira."

*That* made her giddy.

"And I like your laugh. It is like the breeze blowing gently through tiny bells."

"A wind chime," she said. "How poetic, William."

"I enjoy the view of the river from the hilltop. Would that be all right?"

She'd have followed him anywhere right then. "Sure, but I need to tighten my girth first."

"The groomsman—" he began, but by the time he finished offering someone else's services, she'd dropped her stirrup, leaned down, pulled the buckles tighter and had her leg back in position again.

She took one look at his raised eyebrows and grinned at him. "I'm not very good at letting people do everything for me," she confessed.

"So it appears. Your staff in America must have had it quite easy."

She didn't want to get into that. "Let's do that hill now."

Halfway up at the steep, boulder-strewn hill, Chloe's saddle slipped just enough for her to realize her girth had loosened again. She tightened her legs and wondered what kind of substandard equipment they had in this country. She was just reaching for a handful of mane when the saddle tilted to the left, then broke free completely.

The mare panicked and jumped to the right, then whirled on her forehand. Chloe got dumped on the left and tucked into a protective roll that carried her partway down the hill before she stopped. She'd fallen plenty of times in the past; what trick rider hadn't? But rolling over and over left her head spinning when she sat up.

"Moira!"

Not spinning so much, though, that she didn't melt inside when William's arms circled her.

"Hold still," he ordered.

As if she wanted to move while his hands roamed her arms and legs, feeling, she supposed, for broken bones. The thundering in her ears was new, and it took her a moment to realize that it was their escorts charging up to them.

There were queries of "What happened?" and "Are you all right, Your Highness?" and orders of "Someone catch that damned mare!"

But Chloe couldn't have cared less. William's arms were warm and strong and tender as he sat behind her to lend support she didn't need, except for the fact that she found it difficult to breathe with him touching her all over. His chest was hard and solid against her back. His thighs cradled her hips sturdily. His breath teased the top of her head as he gave orders to all the men in a low, controlled voice that did nothing to disguise his fury.

He had the escorts hopping to do his bidding. All Chloe wanted to do was recline in his arms a bit longer. She supposed, though, that she should let him know she was unhurt.

*In another minute.*

The saddle landed at her side, next to William's knee, and William's man-at-arms held the end of the leather girth, where there should have been three buckles.

"All three gave way, Your Majesty. They must have been cut."

"Whattaya mean, cut?" Chloe would have bolted right out of William's arms, except that he held her close.

"Your Highness, you should not move," he warned.

"I'm fine." She reached for the girth and saw remnants of stitching, little pieces of broken threads all that remained on the off side. "Maybe it's dry rot."

"Your Highness...Moira, please be careful," William cautioned. "You might have internal injuries—"

"I'm fine," she snapped, and bolted to her feet. "Is my horse all right?"

"She is fine, Your Highness," an escort answered, and led her forward so that Chloe could see for herself that the mare was neither frightened nor limping.

William followed closely as she circled the mare. "You are limping, Moira. Let me carry you back to the castle now."

Chloe waved his concern away. "I'm fine. If I could have the girth from one of your—"

*Carry me back? As in, ride double?*

"Well, my leg *is* a little sore from that tumble."

William snapped his fingers; his horse was instantly led forward. He mounted from the high side of the hill, then reached for her. A man-at-arms gave her a boost, but she barely felt him touch her leg as William settled her sideways in the saddle, while he himself moved to sit behind it.

They started downhill.

Chloe had ridden in many different positions, but sideways down a steep hill wasn't one of them. As a trick rider, she'd always been in control, but it wasn't possible this way. "Oh, this is awful," she complained with a groan.

"What, Moira?" William asked, his voice warm and husky in her ear. "Am I holding you too tight?"

*Yeah, right.*

"Oh, no, Your Majesty…William."

"What then?"

"Nothing. William…"

"Yes?"

"Would it be all right if I laid my head on your shoulder?"

"Of course."

His neck was warm from the sun, his shirt as soft as chamois. A week ago she'd been a plain ol' American nobody, and this week she was cradled by a hunk of a king who wanted to help people by building a health care facility on top of a hill.

She couldn't help wondering whether it was possible for him to be as interested in her as he was in his people. She wanted him to be, but, given the circumstances into which she'd been thrown—a royal princess where the boy next door was a grown-up monarch—she'd be wise to keep rein on her emotions and see if they could be friends first.

Not that that sounded nearly as interesting as what she was feeling at the moment.

IT WAS just as King Albert had feared. William hated to admit it, but Moira's father might be right. He had said Moira could be in danger if she came home, and William had promised to protect her.

He would not go back on that promise.

She was warm and cozy in the circle of his arms, and silent enough to give him time to think. Had she adjusted her own girth because she was meek and did not want to trouble anyone, or because, as he now suspected, a measure of American independence had rubbed off on her? After all, she had not lain on the ground and wept. She had not winced when he felt for broken bones. She had not begged for a well-sprung carriage to carry her home, or for the immediate presence of a physician.

He could like this new side of Moira, too. As long as she did not try to forestall what he knew was best for their countries.

He guided his stallion past the stable, to the castle entrance where Emma waited.

She greeted them with concern. "Your Highness—"

"We had a little mishap," William told her. He turned over his reins to his groom, slid backward over his horse's hindquarters, then stood beside Moira's knees and reached up for her.

Her eyes were clear and bright, showing no pain, no anger. She rested her hands on his shoulders, slid off the saddle and allowed him to take her weight. Reluctantly he let her slide down in front of him, when he would have preferred to drag her up against his chest and feel her against him again, face-to-face this time. When her feet touched the ground, he held her for another moment to be sure she was steady, but she had no difficulty and did not even pretend to lean on him.

Good, she was fine. Now he was free to find out who was responsible for her "accident."

"Are you all right?" Emma asked her.

"Yes, I just took a little tumble."

"You?" Emma visibly composed herself. "I'll see you to your quarters, then, Your Highness. Just to be certain."

Moira turned and looked up at him with a warm, soft gaze that told him that maybe, in spite of the dangerous accident, he had made inroads toward a friendship with her. An important step.

When he found the man who had nearly put an end to all this, he would not only punish him, he would make him wish for a quick death.

"Thank you, Your Majesty."

He had liked it ever so much better when she called him by his name. But, of course, she was not free to do so at the moment.

"You were very kind to let me ride back with you."

Every so often, she got formal like that. He really preferred the other side of her, the American one that bubbled over with expressions he could not take literally but wanted to hear more of. And he was quite pleased that she had lost some of the shyness she had exhibited with him on the plane.

"It was my pleasure." *If she only knew.* "Your father has invited me for lunch, so I will see you in a little while."

He watched carefully as she took her first steps away from him, to make sure she was not hurt more than she would let on, that she did not stumble and fall. But she really did appear to be all right. Her limp was slight.

It could have been much worse. She could have been killed.

He turned on everyone present and snapped, "Come to the stables and bring everyone who was anywhere near that mare."

It took only minutes; there was no one else for them to go roust out. The groomsman swore the girth had been perfect when he saddled her.

A man-at-arms from Castle Ennsway stepped forward. "Except for a minute, she was never out of my sight, Your Majesty."

"You deserted your post?" William demanded.

At His Majesty's tone, the man blanched. "Her Highness's own assistant secretary asked me for assistance, Your Majesty. I thought—"

"You *thought?*"

"But, Your Majesty—"

William turned abruptly to his man-at-arms. "Throw him in the dungeon."

CHLOE HAD a one-o'clock lunch date with King Albert.

"What would you like to wear?" Angela asked.

"Oh, I don't know. I usually just..." No, she couldn't say she usually just stood in her cramped bedroom and stared into her dark, minuscule closet until the right clothes struck her. Or that she rooted through the hamper for her least dirty tank top. "...pick a color."

"Like blue?"

"Mmm, maybe." She headed for the shower, thinking maybe red would be a nice color today; it would give her courage. When she returned, wrapped in a towel as big as a sheet, she found a blue dress laid out on the bed.

"Is this all right, Your Highness?" Angela asked.

Well, what did it matter, really? Maybe Angela knew that King Albert's favorite color was blue or something. Maybe she was trying, in her own way, to present Chloe in the best light. "Sure."

"I will get you something else."

"This is fine."

"But, you are—" Angela pointed to her own eyebrows "—frowning?"

"It's fine, really."

Angela rushed toward the closet, calling over her shoulder in an eager tone, "I will bring you every color until you like."

Chloe sighed; she really didn't mean to cause more work for anyone. "Red, Angela."

At ten after one, in a scarlet skirt and heels, she was jogging along a stone passageway—she could have sworn she'd been through it just five minutes before, but so many of them looked alike—and muttering to herself about making one wrong turn after another. When she finally found her father's suite, she burst through the doorway.

Everyone turned to face her at her abrupt entrance; William, his smile warm and gentle as he stood next to her father, King Albert, seated at the head of the table with an oxygen tank by his side, Louis nearby, stroking his beard with a hand that bore a long scar across the back. The servants went about their business silently, and William and Louis moved toward their dining chairs.

Nearly out of breath, Chloe tried to look composed as she apologized courteously. "I'm sorry I'm late, Father."

King Albert's smile was feeble, but warm nonetheless. "I understand your fall has put you off schedule."

Sounded good to her, better than *I got lost in the home I grew up in.* "Yes."

"You were not injured?"

"No, Father."

He nodded, as if he were satisfied with that answer. "Come. Sit."

A servant stood behind the chair on her father's right, holding it for her. William, next to her, and Louis, across, stood by theirs and waited for her to be seated. She'd heard about such manners, of course; she'd just never come across them herself.

"I heard your girth broke?" Louis asked.

"Yes."

William's reply was curt. "It was cut."

Louis's eyebrows puckered in great concern. "Cut? But, Moira, who could have cut it? Who knew you were going riding this morning?"

She shrugged. "Just about anyone, I suppose."

"Ah," Louis said. "But who knew you would be using that particular girth?"

Why did these men talk as if it were a conspiracy? "I'm sure the stitching just dry-rotted or something."

Their meal was set before them, a light stew ladled into bread bowls, served on china trimmed in gold. No one had to tell her it was real gold.

Servers continued to circle the table without speaking, pouring white wine into crystal stemware and dishing out hot rolls and cold butter.

King Albert cleared his throat and gained Chloe's, William's, and Louis's attention. "I am quite tired today."

The aroma of Chloe's lunch made her mouth water, but she sat still, her hands folded in her lap, waiting until someone else made the first move.

King Albert spoke slowly. "I had an announcement planned for later, after we dine, but perhaps I should make it now in case—" he coughed a little "—in case I grow too weak."

"But, Your Majesty—" William began.

King Albert held up his hand to stop him.

William persisted. "It can wait until you are stronger."

"Nonsense, William. Why keep my daughter waiting?" King Albert looked warmly at Chloe and smiled.

It was her first clue that this had something directly to do with her, that it was something that William wanted to put off, if the shuttered look on his face was any indication. Suddenly lunch didn't smell so wonderful, but, all the same, she smiled politely in return.

With a shaky hand, King Albert lifted his wineglass

in a salute to Chloe. "Moira, my daughter, I have missed you these past years. I am delighted to have you home again, to see your beautiful smile, to hear your lovely voice." He paused, whether to catch up on his oxygen or to wait for her response, Chloe wasn't certain.

"Thank you, Father."

His eyes glowed for a moment. "Ah, it does my heart good to see you again, to know that you are happy. A father wants his children to be happy, you know."

Some response seemed to be called for again.

She nodded a little.

"That is why," he announced with great pride, "I have arranged for you to marry."

Without thinking, Chloe jumped to her feet. "Marry? But, Father—" Her protest lost its momentum when the heavy chair, its legs caught on the carpet, wouldn't move out of her way and shoved her forward. Her hands shot out to brace herself, she upended her plate and sent stew splattering all over the white tablecloth, dotting it with broth and chunks of vegetables.

William tossed his napkin onto the table as he bolted to his feet beside her. "Your Majesty, please—"

Chloe looked up at him, thinking that the anguish on his face must mirror her own. She turned back to King Albert to plead her case.

*See, William doesn't want you to marry me off to some...some...man.*

"You can't do this!" Chloe felt a moment of guilt when her father paled slightly. "I mean, not without me meeting him. I could never marry someone I didn't love," she said weakly, not because she didn't mean it, but because a uniformed nurse had dashed into the room and now hovered near the old man's shoulder.

King Albert's voice might have been weak, but his intent was firm as he proclaimed, "Moira, it is for your own good. I have already signed the marriage contract."

"No!"

"William will make you a fine husband."

*William?*

The same William she'd gone riding with this morning? As friends? She whirled on him, standing inches from her. He was tall and broad and could have sat her back down with little effort, but she was too stunned by the news to be intimidated by his size. "All the time...you *knew?*"

He had the good grace to smile sheepishly.

Very quietly, to be sure she had this absolutely correct, she asked, "When you asked me to go riding with you yesterday, you'd already signed a contract to marry me?"

"Yes." The slightest of smiles tugged at the corner of his lips, as if he were testing the waters.

"No!" she roared. She wheeled on her chair and kicked it out of her way. He'd known. All the time, he'd known. How dumb could she be? "When?"

"I approached your father months ago."

"And when did you sign the papers?"

"Last week."

She stood toe-to-toe with him. "I've never met anyone so underhanded, so conniving—"

"Please, Moira."

"How *archaic* could you possibly get?"

"Your father and I think—"

"I think, too, buddy. My answer is no."

"But, Moira—"

"And you can take back your horse!"

## Chapter Five

*I'm a princess. I can do whatever I want.*

William bent down, grasped Chloe's chair with one hand and gently righted it by the table. "Please, Moira, sit down."

As mad as she was, she remembered how gentle his hands had been on her after she'd fallen. Feeling betrayed, she folded her arms across her chest and held her ground, unsure whether to be madder at King Albert or King William.

*I'm a princess. I can do whatever I want.*

"We will discuss this," he said softly, as if she were a naughty child.

William won—she was madder at him. All that acting as if he liked her, cared for her. He'd given her a fancy Andalusian mare, for heaven's sake. What was that? A bribe?

"Calmly, rationally."

"I'm a princess."

He grinned. "Yes, I know." He eased the chair in behind her legs until she sat, then scooted both her and the chair up to the table as if she weighed no more than a young child.

When she looked down, it was clear that the servants

had been busy while she was ranting. The soiled table-cloth had been draped and covered with fresh white napkins. A server hovered nearby with another helping, though from the look on his face, he wasn't certain whether to put it anywhere within her reach.

She had everyone's attention—everyone who mattered. "And, as a princess, I can do whatever I want."

William scooted in beside her and draped his arm along the back of her chair. "Well, in most circumstances."

She turned and batted his arm away. "This is one of them."

"No—"

King Albert interrupted. "The contract is signed. I will hear no more of it."

"I will not marry this man."

"You will."

"Not!"

Her father cast a rueful smile at William. "I am afraid my daughter—" He coughed, and couldn't stop. The nurse took his pulse, adjusted his oxygen cannula, told him to calm himself, and still he coughed.

Prince Louis spoke up. "I feel I must voice my concern."

*Oh, great.*

"My sister has grown up in another country and become quite...headstrong. I think it would be unfair to expect William to put up with her, Father."

"Thanks," Chloe muttered. "I think." It was quite a change from the sniping Louis had done yesterday, and she wished she knew him better. Or at least more about his and Moira's relationship.

King Albert's lips turned gray, and Chloe wouldn't say anything more to upset him. If he'd looked like death warmed over yesterday, he looked halfway in the grave today.

She rose to her feet, carefully this time. "I can see that my behavior is distressing my father. Excuse me, please."

On her way out the door, she told the nearest footman to summon Emma. Chloe needed her more than ever, needed her advice before going one-on-one in a royal battle of wits with William.

WILLIAM FELT MORE ALONE than he had in a long time. Moira had left the dining room abruptly, King Albert had been wheeled off to his bedchamber by his nurse, and Louis had followed.

He had known it was too soon to tell Moira, had begged King Albert to wait, but the old man was concerned about his health and did not want to delay.

There was only one thing William could do now. He had to talk to Moira and explain everything to her, reason with her, convince her that this was in her best interest.

That decided, he rose to his feet.

"His Majesty wishes to speak to you, Your Majesty," the nurse announced from the doorway through which she had taken King Albert.

He strode into the bedchamber to find the old man's eyes closed, Louis bending solicitously over him.

"He is sleeping now," Louis said.

The nurse frowned. "But he sounded so determined." She checked his pulse and oxygen flow.

"Yes, well," Louis said, "you can see he is asleep. Perhaps later, William."

Frustrated by the delay, William grabbed the first

servant he found. "Take me to Her Highness's suite at once."

All the way there, he wondered what he would say, what he *could* say, to change her mind. He could not promise her love or happiness; he knew only that they must marry. And soon.

He was standing outside Moira's door, knocking on it, when she stormed around the corner at the other end of the passageway. "Moira—"

She breezed past him and slammed the door in his face, something no one had ever done before. He grinned and made a mental note to thank King Albert for sending his daughter to live in America; she had picked up such...charming habits there.

He heard other doors within the suite slam, also. She was nothing like the rest of her family, neither spineless nor meek.

*How could I ever have thought so?*

He would consider himself a lucky man if he could get her to the altar. When he had signed the marriage contract, he had done it for his country. It seemed he was to be rewarded.

He rapped his knuckles on the wood again. "Moira, open the door." He tested it and found it opened only a fraction; she had blocked it with something, probably a chair.

A loud crash sounded from within, as if she were tearing the walls down. Literally.

"Moira?" He pressed his ear to the door, but instead of her voice, all he heard were a few more heavy thuds, like stones falling. "Moira, answer me! Are you all right?"

*Dear God, let her be all right.*

He tested the door again, but it still opened only a

fraction. And through that gap, he saw a cloud of dust or smoke coming from her bedchamber. *I will do better next time. I will keep her safe.*

*If she is alive.*

He shoved the door with his shoulder and made no progress. He planted one good, solid kick against it, and heard no more than a small crack. The wood was thick and braced, and it seemed that an eternity passed before his efforts finally crushed the chair she had tipped beneath the knob.

The double doors to her bedchamber were slightly ajar. Dust poured out through them, and he saw only rubble beyond.

He heard her coughing, a hacking, torturous distress signal that tore at his heart. "Moira!"

He crossed the sitting room in bounds and threw open the double doors. Along the far wall was a pile of stones and rubble. A huge hole gaped overhead.

Moira sat slumped against a chair, one hand waving dust away from her face as she stared at the mess in front of her.

He knelt beside her, his hands moving rapidly over her body, looking for injury, even though he could plainly see not a scratch on her, no stones lying around her body, no blood.

He said a silent prayer of thanks.

"It was such a pretty bed," she said.

"There is a bed under there?"

She nodded. "A canopy bed. I always wanted a canopy bed." She cast a startled glance his way. "I mean, in the United States, I missed having a canopy bed."

With more time to look at the mess, he could see a chandelier lying amid the plaster and stone, too.

"Two attempts on your life in one day, Moira—"

She halted him with a gentle laugh. "Oh, stop. It was an accident, William. I mean, how many years has that thing been hanging there, anyway?"

"It should not have fallen."

"Well, you won't get any argument there."

Accidental or intentional, it made no difference to William. He could not protect her if he was not beside her.

"Are you all right? Can you walk?" He was quick to lend her his hand to rise.

She brushed plaster dust off herself. He wanted to help, so he did. He began with her back; she could not object to that. Then he picked bits and pieces out of her hair, until she pulled out her braid, bent over and swung her hair loose and free.

"How's that?" she asked, her back still to him as she straightened.

He sank his fingers into her tresses. "Much better."

She looked over her shoulder at him. "William?"

He busied himself with brushing imaginary debris off her shoulders. He worked his way down and around, over her skirt, lingered on her knees.

"William." She sounded…out of breath.

He stood up again, in front of her this time, his chest nearly touching her breasts, when what he wanted to do was crush her to him. Her eyes were soft, confused, liquid warmth compared to the cold rubble around them. Had this happened at night, she would have been buried beneath it.

Leonard had advised him to romance Moira. It seemed stronger methods were mandatory if he was to keep her alive long enough to get her to the altar.

"I have decided," he said. "You are coming home with me."

WILLIAM, arms folded across his chest, stood by the door and watched as Moira's maid packed for her.

"Angela, stop that," Moira ordered.

"Let her be, Your Highness," he reiterated for the hundredth time. For a princess, she certainly did not know when to obey her superiors. He was beginning to have mixed feelings about her stay in the United States. He would bet that American friend of hers, that Chloe Something-or-Other, had been a bad influence.

Moira stomped up to him until they were toe-to-toe. Inside, he wished for her to come closer.

"Angela is my maid."

"Yes, I know. That is why she is packing your clothes."

"She is *my* maid." She gritted out the words. "Why the hell is she taking orders from you?"

He could not stop his grin, and he saw a fire light in her eyes in response. She was a very passionate woman. He did his best to contain his amusement, lest he anger her more. "Because she knows when we are married, I will be her king."

Very slowly and clearly, she said, "That will never happen." She returned to the closet, pulled folded jeans from one of the two trunks the maid was packing and tossed them back onto the shelf. Several more pairs followed.

"Stop that," he ordered.

Not only did she not stop, but she tossed sweaters and nightgowns and lingerie over her shoulders with no order as to where they landed.

"Stop that, or you will have nothing to wear."

That did not stop her, but it did give him pause as he visualized Moira in his castle without a stitch of clothing on.

She glanced up at him with a sly smile. "Cat got your tongue?"

Composing himself was not easy, until he remembered that her life was in danger. He took her by the hand. "Come, Moira. Your maid can send the trunks later."

She dug in her feet, but he tugged her along behind him as if she weighed no more than a pillow.

"Wait, Emma hasn't come yet."

"Perhaps she grew tired of your headstrong ways and quit."

She grabbed a door frame and hung on. "But she wouldn't do that."

He pried her fingers free, all the while knowing he should be aggravated with her, but feeling the excitement of sparring with a worthy opponent. "I would not be so sure."

"You don't understand. I *need* her. Now."

She grabbed the opposite frame with her other hand, and he made short work of that one, too.

"Your brother hired you a perfectly good new secretary."

"I need the old one."

As they traveled down the stone passageways, William was aware that this was not the picture he wanted to present to prying eyes—the king towing his future queen. He stopped and faced her head-on. "Moira—"

"William, please—"

He modulated his tone. "Moira, listen to me."

She opened her mouth to object; he wanted to kiss it quiet.

"Listen," he said, and his voice sounded ragged even to him. "I will find Emma for you, if..."

She quit struggling, and he realized that, with his

hands grasping her wrists as they were, he had dragged her up against his chest. Unfortunately, their hands were between them. He promised himself he would do it properly later.

"If you will get in my car without a fuss and wait for me."

"But—"

"Without a fuss."

"I need—"

"*I* need *you* to be safe. If Emma is here, I will find her. I promise."

CHLOE WAITED in William's Mercedes, though not patiently. She stewed.

What would a princess do in a situation like this? Well, this had probably never happened before in the twentieth century. So what would a princess of old have done? Given in or gotten tough?

She wished she could call Moira and ask her advice. Emma would advise Chloe what to do, of course, but Moira would tell her what a princess would *want* to do. And Chloe didn't think it would be so different from what she was thinking.

She'd get tough—in a princessy sort of way, of course. Moira had said not to be sassy, but that was her, not Chloe.

She wondered how Moira's new life was going. She'd be looking for a job, a totally new concept for a woman who'd been born with a silver spoon in her mouth. Chloe peered out the window at the castle and amended that to a gold spoon. Encrusted with diamonds, no doubt. What did Moira know about working?

What did Chloe know about princessing?

William was bigger than she. She'd wait in the car until he found Emma, then she'd go to Baesland Castle with him and make his life unbearable until he agreed to send her back home and court her properly. It occurred to her that she'd spent only one night in Castle Ennsway and already she thought of it as home. She was coming along with this princess thing just fine.

As for the marriage contract, William was a king, a monarch, for heaven's sake. The college courses she'd had over the past ten years were mainly in science. If it had offered a lab or field trips, she'd taken it. Not once had she enrolled in anything remotely connected to the study of law, but common sense about how a monarchy worked told her William could void the contract if she talked her father into doing the same.

It all would have been so much simpler if she weren't attracted to him. If he wasn't Prince Charming all grown up. If she didn't get so darned confused every time he touched her. She needed to remember to breathe whenever she got near him.

Trouble was, she had a poor memory.

She'd admired his plan to build a health care facility. Now it made sense why *he* was planning it in *her* country. Sort of. But she wasn't about to marry him because of a contract. She had good ol' American pride, after all.

William came out the door of the great hall, jogged down the stone steps and crossed around to the other side of the car. She didn't look at him as he got in and sat beside her. She knew how big and strong and exciting he looked, and she refused to be swayed.

"Home," he said to the driver, who started the engine.

"Wait!"

The driver did nothing of the kind.

"What about Emma?"

William reached over to her lap and took her hand in his. She snatched it back.

"I regret to tell you that Emma was dismissed late this morning."

"What?"

"She left the castle immediately."

"She's gone?"

He nodded.

No Emma? But Emma knew all the rules, the etiquette, the truth…

Chloe stared straight ahead. How would she cope with William now?

# Chapter Six

William expected Moira to jump out of the Mercedes and storm back to Castle Ennsway. Such fire! Such spirit!

Instead, she huddled in the corner by the door, her eyes steadfastly turned away from him, her knuckles white where her hands, fingers laced together, lay in her lap.

"Emma is *my* secretary." Her voice was barely audible, and he had to tip his head toward her. What he managed to hear still carried strength of conviction, still rang of American ego, which was famous for always wanting to come out on top. "Who told her to leave?"

"Louis said your father dismissed her."

"He had no right."

"I am sorry, Moira. But he *is* the king."

"I think I would like to withdraw my permission for you to address me by my name."

"Very well. Until we are married—"

"We're not getting married."

She did not even snap at him. He understood her animosity; he had wanted to break the wedding news to her more gently. After he met her, he had wished for her to desire him before she learned of the marriage contract, wished for her to care for him in such a way that it would be like an answer to a dream. He understood that she felt lost after so many years in another country.

But he could not understand her confusion over this matter. She was a royal princess, born into a monarchy. She knew she had to do what was expected of her, what her father ordered, what was best for her and their two countries.

All the same, he wanted to comfort her. He yearned for her to look at him again as if she would like to devour him, as she had this morning during their ride. If she would just look at him...

If she would not accept his physical comfort, he would give her what he could. "I requested every Ennsway man-at-arms be sent out to find Emma. Louis has seen to it. When we reach Baesland Castle, I will deploy my men-at-arms, also. If she is here, they will find her."

"Check the next flight to Texas."

"Texas?"

"Emma and...Chloe are quite close. She might go there."

CHLOE STARED out the window as they retraced the road they'd taken yesterday from Baesland Airport to Ennsway Castle. It was safer than looking at William. He sat too close to her as it was. She could feel warmth from his thigh near hers, and it distracted her. She couldn't scoot any closer to the door; she was practically glued to it already.

"Could I have a little more room?"

"Certainly." The temperature dropped as he moved

away, until he reached over, grabbed her hand and tugged her toward him.

"What are you doing?"

"You requested more room, but you are not making use of it."

She pulled her hand free. "I just need it for space."

"Space?"

"Yes, don't you ever need your space?" Look who she was asking—a man who lived in a castle and lorded over people. "Oh, I guess not. Never mind."

*I'll just sit here and try to forget that I can still feel your hand on mine.*

Outside the Mercedes, farmland merged into rolling foothills. Foothills gave way to tree-covered slopes. Slopes angled into the mountain itself. She hadn't noticed it the day before, but there were definite differences between the two countries other than topography.

The condition of the pavement, for one, improved when they crossed the border; it was newer, wider, smoother. Automobiles in Ennsway were fewer, older, darker, utilitarian; in Baesland they were newer, nicer, with a few bright Porsches and luxurious Bentleys sprinkled in.

Baesland City flanked the main road, rivaling San Francisco for the aerobic benefits of walking from shop to shop. The pedestrians were better dressed than most of the people who had come to see her at the airport.

Her father, confined to the castle due to his health, needed some fresh input on running his country. She wondered what the heck Louis had been doing about that, if anything. Why should Ennsway be run-down compared to Baesland?

If King Albert thought she was some timid little creature who would be married off to the nearest king, he had a rude awakening coming. And if he thought she was going to keep silent about his not treating the people as well as their neighbors' king treated his, he'd better be prepared for some hard truths.

They turned off the route to the airport and headed higher. The road snaked upward from one hairpin turn to another, lined by forest, allowing glimpses only from time to time of a stone fortress perched high above them. If Ennsway Castle had been bigger and grander than anything Moira had ever seen, then Baesland Castle, as they drove closer, was breathtaking.

Chloe couldn't help herself—she craned her head by the window for a better view. *This* was a castle straight out of a fairy tale. *This* was surely where Cinderella had ended up.

"Do you like it?" William asked softly, even with a bit of uncertainty, as if this were a very important question for him.

"What's not to like? Other than I'm being brought here against my will."

He smiled—not the result she'd been hoping for.

The final approach to the castle was a long, straight drive, giving Chloe a remarkable view. She suspected she'd seen this castle on calendars.

"You have a moat?" It circled the curtain wall, which had all the requisite battlements and towers, just more of them than seemed possible.

"It is the same moat that you tried to swim across as a child."

Mentally she slapped herself upside the head. *Careful!* "I don't remember it being so wide."

"How odd. Adults normally remember things as being larger than they actually were in their childhood."

"Uh, yeah, I usually do, too."

"Now that you are all grown up..."

She was pleased to hear a catch in his voice.

"...you will understand why our mothers were so upset. Imagine, a little girl who thought she could swim farther than a cannonball could fly."

Chloe had sudden insight into Moira as a child, and it didn't quite mesh with the reserved young woman she'd met at a charity horse show ten years ago. Cool, collected, soft-spoken Princess Moira had hooked a two-foot-long blue ribbon to the bridle on Chloe's borrowed horse, shaken her hand and congratulated her. At the time, Chloe had been pretty darned impressed that she'd shaken hands with a real princess.

When they ran into each other again on UCSB's campus, they'd struck up a conversation. The rest was history. Even though, as their friendship solidified, Moira had proposed that they trade places a couple of times for an occasional weekend, Chloe hadn't thought of her as adventurous.

That image was up for reassessment.

The chauffeur drove through a stone gatehouse, complete with portcullis and murder holes, across the one-lane bridge over the moat and through another gatehouse. If she'd been a princess of old, she would have worried that escape from here would be impossible. That didn't bother the modern her in the least, because she wouldn't have to escape; if she succeeded in annoying him enough, William would eventually send her away.

Though finding him in such a monstrosity might be difficult. So much for her idea of leaving clothes and dirty dishes strewn all around the place. Even if the servants didn't pick them up immediately, the chances of William coming across them in the next six months would be slim indeed. And she had no intention of being here that long.

"This is much larger than my father's castle, isn't it?"

"There are three hundred rooms here, more if you want to count the others."

She'd been right; he couldn't have any concept of needing space. "Others?"

He shrugged. "The greenhouse, the aviary, the indoor pool, the theater..."

"Oh, those."

In the bailey, the tires crunched on gravel as they rounded the reflecting pool, complete with a pair of white swans paddling about. A curved, double staircase—obviously added after the threat of castle-storming was over—led up to a stained-glass doorway that would have done any cathedral proud. On either side were pots of ivy-shrouded sculptures.

The chauffeur hopped out and held Chloe's door open. William, she noted, was quick to round the car and hold out his hand. Though her fingers itched to touch his again, she pointedly ignored the gesture.

"What possible use could anyone have for three hundred rooms?"

"It will not seem like so many when our children are grown. Please, come this way."

"Our children?"

"I must have an heir. Surely you did not think we would not—"

Her hand shot up to stop him in midsentence. If she were the fainting type, those words would have brought on a spell. Mercifully, he didn't find the need to lay it all out in words. She'd entertained thoughts along those lines during their ride this morning, but not since being informed that they *had* to get married.

On the stairs, he grinned and held out his elbow for her. "Yes, I think you understand."

She declined his arm and ascended without him. "If we *were* to get married—" she left no room for doubt about that not happening in this lifetime "—even children don't take up that much room."

He kept pace with her. "Oh, but they will need quite large apartments as they reach adulthood."

"Apartments?"

"Yes. Mine is thirty rooms. They will each have—"

"Wait. Stop. Let me get this straight. You live in a thirty-room apartment in this castle?"

"If you find it too small, I shall have it enlarged."

"I won't even see it."

"Very well. There is a nice apartment that I hope you will like. It is near mine."

*The better to annoy you, my dear.* A blaring stereo, perhaps, would be a good start.

"It is smaller, though. Only twenty-five rooms."

Chloe couldn't help herself; she laughed. The poor man hadn't a clue how much American ingenuity she possessed.

Yet.

Another car pulled up behind the one they'd just exited.

"Ah, your clothes have arrived. Good. You will be able to dress in time."

"In time for what?"

"Dinner."

Inside the entry hall, she gave up trying not to look like a tourist. Let William think she had a short-term memory if he wanted. As long as she had to be here, she was going to enjoy her prison. Much larger than her father's, the entry had a black-and-white marble floor, so highly polished that it appeared no one ever walked on it. On the wall were two large, dark portraits. She stepped closer to them and searched her memory for facts she'd learned long ago in art appreciation.

"Rembrandt?" she whispered reverently.

"Yes. I thought they belonged here rather than lost among the others in the east gallery."

They had his eyes, the men in those two paintings, though William's were warmer and twinkled with his sense of humor. The same straight nose, though they were looking down theirs as if they were gods and she were lower than a peon. William was obstinate about the marriage agreement he'd made with King Albert, but he hadn't stooped to looking down his royal nose at her.

Good thing, too. Of course, that might be because he thought she was as royal as he.

Even if she hadn't been raised in foster homes, she couldn't have imagined her ancestors ever having portraits done of themselves, much less by Rembrandt.

William spoke with his secretary, then returned to Chloe's side. "Leonard will have someone here shortly to show you to your apartment. Dinner with the prime minister is in one hour."

*The prime minister?*

She needed Emma sooner than she'd thought. Chloe hadn't a clue what a princess wore to dinner in the neighboring king's castle, with or without a prime minister in attendance. It was Emma's job to tell her what Moira would already know, like how to address the man, what kind of small talk to make—all stuff that had not been covered in any of Chloe's years of college courses. For heaven's sake, she didn't even know whether she—as Moira—had ever met the man before. For all she knew, he might be another old family friend.

She debated faking a headache, but there was no need. Her head was positively spinning. She had no choice but to put her foot down until Emma returned.

"EXCUSE ME," William begged of the prime minister. "I must check on Her Royal Highness."

It was the stupidest excuse he had ever offered. Hell, it might have been the *only* excuse he had ever uttered, but he wanted Moira present—now!—and he knew he was not going to get his wish unless he retrieved her himself. She had already told Leonard she could not make it tonight, and Leonard had also reported that she had dismissed her maid for the evening.

The prime minister had been eyeing him speculatively for the past hour, and William could not stand it anymore. Ordinarily, someone would have handled this task for him. A man-at-arms was looking like a good choice for the job. This evening, though, he took it on himself and got a good dose of just how big his castle was by how long it took him to reach Moira's apartment.

With the flat side of his fist he pounded on the door, wasting no time with social amenities.

"Who is it?" floated softly from inside.

"You know damn well—" He took a deep breath and needlessly tugged his suit coat into submission. "It is William, Your Highness."

"I've retired for the evening, Your Majesty."

He had hoped she would revert to his name, but it

appeared it was not to be so tonight. "Open the blasted—" Again, he paused. He raked his fingers through his hair. He had never done that before. Now he understood the emotion behind it when he'd seen other men do it. "May I come in?"

He pressed his ear up to the wood to hear whether she was laughing. He liked her laugh. A lot. Too much, perhaps, because he should have kicked the door open and dragged her kicking and screaming to dinner. Instead, he heard music, and not with a beat he imagined anyone would "retire" to.

"Yes, come in."

He pushed the door open to a scene he had never had the foresight to imagine. Moira, her blond hair in a high, bouncy ponytail, a fuzzy peach-colored sweatband around her forehead, a pretty pink flush to her face as she stretched first one arm up over her head, then the other. Over and over, she kept time with the music. The cropped hem of her matching shirt rose with her arm, giving him a glimpse of bare midriff before the hem dropped and covered her again.

Glimpse. Cover. Glimpse. Cover.

With a sweep of his hand, he indicated her attire. "What the hell is that?"

She looked down at herself, but continued exercising as she counted, "Nineteen...and...twenty. Sweats," she replied, then placed her hands on her hips and bent sideways. "One and two and..."

"I know what sweats are." Was that growl coming from him? "What are you doing in them? Why are you——? Stop that!" He strode across the room and punched the volume button off.

She came to an abrupt halt, which sent her ponytail

jiggling down to a slower stop. He wanted to go over to her and bat it and get it bouncing again.

"I'm exercising."

"I can see that. The question is, why are you doing that when you were expected at dinner an hour ago?"

She bent down and stretched her fingers beyond her toes, laying her hands flat on the floor, giving him time to study the tiny bumps that made up her lower spine. "Didn't Leonard tell you I have a headache?"

"I will send you some aspirin."

"I don't take medicine."

He was so surprised, he got sidetracked. "Never?"

"Nope. My physiology professor had us do experiments that convinced me I don't want to mess with drugs." She stood upright, then bent over backward, arching her body until her hands touched down on the floor behind her feet.

William's mouth went dry. If she would stretch just a little bit farther, he would find out whether she was wearing a bra. And whether it was peach-colored, too. He was unable to think coherently until she righted herself. And, while he waited with bated breath, his annoyance ebbed. He wondered whether she was deliberately teasing him, but, if this is how she chose to do it, he did not care.

"You must come to dinner at once."

"Are you all right? You sound a bit hoarse."

"I have a guest waiting. I am upset that you did not come to dinner."

She rose and, with her sleeve, blotted a drop of sweat amid the tendrils of hair sweeping her neck. "Okay. Lead the way."

"You are not dressed properly."

"Oh, well, if you want me to dress *properly,* I'd need Emma to pick out something appropriate for me."

"That is your maid's job."

"I dismissed her for the night."

"Ah, yes." So this was how she wanted it to be. He grinned. "Very well." He found the closet on his third attempt, and selected a pale green dress. "Put this on."

"Not my color."

"Your what?"

"It's not my color. I don't look good in it."

"Then why do you have it?"

She shrugged. "A mistake?"

He selected a camel-colored dress and shoved it into her hands.

She held it up and looked at it as if she had never seen it before. "Nice."

"I am happy it meets with your approval. Get dressed."

"I need shoes."

He had second thoughts about wanting to marry her. He searched through the shelves, selected a pair of high heels and slapped them into her hands. "There. I will expect you in ten minutes."

"Jewelry?"

"You do not need any."

She fingered one earlobe. "I don't know. I think I'd feel naked without earrings."

He thought she ought not to say "naked" to a man who wanted to take her in his arms and kiss her senseless. "Where are your jewels?" he demanded.

She made a face that was certainly supposed to be puzzled, but he could only think of it as cute. Not something he needed to be thinking just now.

"Then you will have to do without earrings until your maid arrives tomorrow."

"Mmm, I guess I could."

*Finally!*

"But I need someone to do my hair."

Never had he met anyone so exasperating. Not as a prince, and certainly not in all his ten years as king. "Would you like me to dress you, too?"

He must have caught her off guard, because she did not have a snappy retort to that stupid question. He did not particularly care how she took it—he might as well have sentenced himself to the torture chamber for all the distress that threat gave him.

Lifting her sweatshirt off over her head, seeing more of the tanned skin beneath, finding out if she wore a bra. Then pulling her sweatpants down around her ankles, allowing her to kick them off. This was how he would undress her. And, once he got that far, he did not think he would be able to bear covering her up with more clothing. Not immediately.

He hoped to hell she did not accept his dare, or the prime minister would be dining alone.

CHLOE could have called his bluff and let him dress her, but she wasn't ready for all that entailed. Once he made the offer, his eyes had turned the darkest shade of blue she'd ever seen. She wasn't ready for what he had to offer. Not if she wanted to leave this castle a single woman.

Without another word, he turned abruptly and fled her apartment.

So, she couldn't call his bluff. That left possibly making a fool of herself in front of his dinner guest. All she could do was summon up some good ol' American spunk and make do. Perhaps choose her words carefully, so as not to indicate whether she thought they'd met before or not.

But she was tired of thinking all the time before she spoke, of racking her brain for the best, most tactful, most demure way of phrasing everything. Emma had said to be herself, that her American ways were part of her charm over here.

Okay, she could do that.

She stripped, washed, brushed and dressed in fifteen minutes, all the while wondering where Emma had gone. Without her, Chloe had no one to look to for dependable advice. Was Emma in Texas with Moira, helping her, when she should be here?

A maid was waiting in the hall outside Chloe's door. "I will show you the way to the dining room, Your Highness." Her English was far better than Angela's.

Chloe thought the rather large, unsmiling woman was more of an escort than a leader. Which bothered her not a bit.

Their route seemed to be a shortcut. Instead of the wide, well-lit passageways she'd taken to reach her apartment in the first place, she was led along plain narrow passageways and down winding neweled staircases with no handrails for support if she got dizzy.

"Your Highness," the maid said as she approached a wide doorway and stepped to the side.

Inside, Chloe surveyed a room that surely must have been a chapel at one time. Three-story ceiling arches of cut granite that had to have employed a mason for years, dark wood between them, heavily leaded windows towering in the far wall. The dining table, with all its china and crystal and candles, looked lost in the center of the carpet in the long, narrow room.

William and his guest waited in wall chairs pulled at angles to the hearth, though there was no fire. Alone, Chloe thought, the prime minister would be considered a handsome man. Well dressed. Sophisticated-looking. However, next to William's broad shoulders and carved features—just a touch of ruggedness to add character—he paled in comparison.

Should she address him as "Sir," or "Mr. Prime Minister," or "Mr. X"? If she used no form of address at all, would it be as bad as using an incorrect one?

*What a lot of phony brouhaha.*

She'd gotten through her first twenty-eight years without these worries. Why not the next twenty-eight, too?

When she stepped into the room, William and the prime minister rose immediately to their feet and set their drinks on a side table.

She took a deep breath and remembered to be herself. Careful not to let a high heel tangle in the fringe on the edge, she walked across the carpet to the two men, smiled, extended her hand and said, "Hi. How're y'all doin'?"

# Chapter Seven

Much to William's amusement, the neighboring prime minister remained at Baesland Castle for three days.

"Her Highness is such a breath of fresh air," he said with a toothy smile the first day, right after the princess dismissed her correct style as so much "royal brouhaha" and told him he could use her given name, Moira.

William could not argue with that assessment. He could add so much more about her, but nothing he wanted to share.

"I want to practice my English with her" was the excuse the prime minister gave for remaining a second day.

"Your English is fine," William pointed out. If anyone was to practice their English with her, he wanted to be the one. He wanted to go riding with her again. He toyed with the idea of challenging her to another swim in his moat.

Late in the third day, the prime minister was summoned to the telephone for an unexpected, unexplained phone call that William had ordered Leonard to manufacture. The prime minister departed soon afterward, leaving William to dine alone this morning with Moira.

*At last!*

As he went in search of her, he carried two things with him. The first was a folder filled with sketches of wedding gowns submitted overnight by various designers, all vying for the privilege of making Her Highness's dress for the wedding of the century. The sooner she chose, the better. For many reasons. One was her safety. Another was his imagination, which had been spinning quite elaborate fantasies involving the two of them alone in his suite for an entire night.

And in the pocket of his jacket, nestled in a burgundy velvet box bearing the Baesland insignia, was a gold engagement ring. After signing the marriage contract, William had selected small rubies, emeralds, and diamonds, passed down from generation to generation of ancestral queens, and had them reset. The design was a unique melding of two slightly different crowns, representing the unification of Baesland and Ennsway which would take place, by agreement with King Albert, on their wedding day.

Moira had neither done nor said anything to indicate that she would accept the ring. He carried it with him every day so that he would have it when the perfect time arrived. That would be either when she came to her senses or when he charmed her into it.

As for getting her to choose a dress designer, he was about to discover whether that would require charm or chicanery.

He found her, not in the atrium where they had dined for the past three mornings with the prime minister—and where she had perpetually shown up late—but eating breakfast alone in her own apartment, at a table by a sunny window. He figured her tardiness was designed to annoy him, but, in fact, it only made him anticipate her arrival more.

"Good morning, Your Highness."

"Your Majesty."

While her greeting was not unpleasant, he suspected the ring would remain in his pocket today. "I have brought sketches for you from the best designers in Europe."

"Leave them on the table."

Boldly he pulled out a chair and seated himself adjacent to her. "Thank you. I would love to join you."

She did not bolt.

Assured that she did not find his presence intolerable, he opened the folder and spread out eight sketches. The white tablecloth was hand-embroidered with bouquets of red roses, and he hoped its subliminal message would put her in the right mood.

"What are these?" she asked.

"Wedding gowns."

"Let me rephrase the question." She stirred her tea with more agitation than necessary, and the spoon pinged repeatedly against the inside of the cup. "Why are they *here?*"

"For you to choose a designer. If one of these—"

"I don't think I should choose a dress before I choose a husband, do you?"

"Is that how it is done in America?"

"Yes."

"Young girls there do not read magazines and dream of their gowns from the time they are old enough to walk?"

"Certainly not." She raised her cup, blew on it gently and took a tiny sip to test the temperature.

"I think you are lying."

"I think you're behind the times."

Fingers outstretched, he made minor adjustments to the layout of the sketches, in order to draw her attention back to them. "Please choose one."

She spared them a glance. "Do you have pop-ups in this country?"

"Pop-ups?"

"Yeah, they're a breakfast food."

"I have never heard of them."

"You toast them in the toaster. You do have toasters, don't you?"

With a shrug, he told the truth. "I have no idea. But, please, the sketches. You do not find the slightest admiration for the talent of any one of these designers?"

She shook her head. "Sorry, I just can't think without my pop-ups." She sipped more tea.

"I will see what my chef can do."

Many of the gowns were very traditional, but some were, to put it kindly, typically designer-innovative. He selected one he thought particularly hideous—it would be a crime to cover her lovely curves in such a sack—and slid it toward her until it touched her rose-rimmed plate.

"I think this one suits you," he said.

"You'd have to lock me in the tower first."

A tiny crease puckered above the bridge of her nose, and he wanted to reach up with his finger and erase it. But if his hand got that far without her batting it away, he knew he would not stop there. He would slide it across her cheek to see whether her skin was as soft as it looked. His fingers would wander on their own, over her jawline, brush across her ear and wind into her hair, which she had left down.

He liked it down—so much more "her" than that stuffy French braid.

"Really?" He strove to sound as if he were surprised. "You do not like it?"

"If I died and someone buried me in that one, I'd come back to life just to hurt them."

"I see." He did his best to appear thoughtful; frowned a little, pursed his lips a little, stared at the sketches for a full minute. He pointed toward another. "Perhaps this one then?"

"For a man who dresses as well as you do, you have abominable taste in wedding gowns."

"You think I dress well?"

She looked away, but not before her cheeks pinkened. If she was trying to annoy him by being difficult, William thought, she was doing more suffering than he.

He held up a different sketch. "This one?"

"Terrible."

"Yes, I thought so, too."

He went through them one by one, gauging her expressions, noting her adjectives. Only one escaped an instant rejection, though rejection was not long in coming.

"No, that one would never do." She bolted to her feet. "Excuse me, please. My father is expecting me this morning."

And he knew her reply had been delayed because that was the gown she would have wanted, had she gotten to choose her husband.

Humming softly, William left her apartment and handed the folder to Leonard. "The one on top. Have the designer begin immediately."

"They will need to measure Her Highness. And I am not certain her secretary would keep your secret."

"Send someone to her maid, then. Tell her it is to update her wardrobe."

Leonard bowed slightly. "Ingenious, Your Majesty. She does not want to see more sketches from this designer?"

"No, she appeared to like that particular gown very much."

As did he. Better yet, he was going to like her in it.

IF the wedding dress turned out half as pretty as the sketch, Chloe knew it would be exquisite.

On someone else.

It was only a small drawing, and on it she couldn't tell embroidery from pearls, but the offset shoulders, narrow bodice, full skirt and long train were enough to make a gal want to marry the first king who proposed.

Trouble was, William was the only king she was ever likely to be interested in, he hadn't proposed, and she had her own archaic notions about marrying for love.

"The chauffeur has brought the car around, Your Highness."

"Thank you, Humphrey."

As a private secretary, Humphrey, the man hired by Prince Louis and formerly bumped down to Emma's assistant, was efficient. He'd stepped into Emma's job the morning following her disappearance. Her on-the-surface job, that is, not the position of constant support and bottomless well of information that Chloe truly needed.

"That's all for now, Humphrey."

"As you wish." He disappeared as silently as he'd arrived.

Chloe, on today's trek through Baesland Castle, only had to stop twice to ask servants for directions before she found the entry hall. As she entered it from the north, William strolled in from the south. She got the distinct impression he'd been waiting for her, and it gave her heart a little flip-flop.

"Ah, there you are, Your Highness." He'd been very diligent in not using her name. Moira's name. "I did not hear your music this morning."

"Did you miss it, Your Majesty?" She missed hearing his name on her lips, but she'd started this and she was going to see it through until she was a free woman again.

After she had time to calm down and think rationally, she'd realized that all she had to do to prevent the wedding was to announce her true identity. *She* wasn't the owner of the name on the contract. *She* wasn't the princess William had bargained for. *She* wasn't the daughter Albert had signed away. But she truly wanted to stay a princess, and there was only one way to do that *and* avoid getting sold up the river, and that was to stick to her plan and get William to send her packing.

"Because if you missed it, I'll be certain to play it soon."

Not that it would do any good. No matter how loudly she played it the past three mornings, endangering her own hearing in the process, he hadn't complained. She doubted much noise had actually penetrated the thick stone walls between her apartment and his.

*Pity.*

She made a beeline for the stained-glass door. "My

father is waiting.'' Maybe she could talk him into voiding his part of the contract first.

"Your Highness, may I have a moment of your time? I shall see that you are not very late.'' He waited only a moment before adding, "In the small drawing room? Please, it is very important.''

Perhaps he'd already rethought the whole issue. Maybe her music had reached his apartment, after all, and driven him out of it. Curious, she followed him through a corner of the great room and into the drawing room, which might have been small by castle standards, but was still far from cozy.

"I have a question about the ceremony.''

*So much for his rethinking skills.* "I hope you're not talking about a wedding ceremony.''

"But of course.''

She fisted her hands on her hips. "Yours and whose?''

She'd done everything she could think of to wear him down. She'd blasted the stereo at odd hours, perpetually arrived late for meals, refused to pick a dress designer, turned down his invitations to go riding. That last one had been difficult, but fighting for her independence required tough measures.

Not only had William not worn down, he still had that darned twinkle in his eyes. Though he was careful to mask it just enough that she couldn't call him on it.

"Yours and mine, Moira.''

Her name on his lips sounded just as sweet as it had when she first gave her permission to use it. "I told you—''

"Ah, here she is!''

Chloe followed his gaze, turned toward the door and saw Emma, smiling as if she'd missed her. "Emma!''

"Your Highness."

Relieved to see her again, Chloe threw her arms around the older woman's neck and hugged her close.

*My ally. My faithful friend, who will stand by me and tell everyone that I was raised in the United States, and it's unfair to force me to marry.*

"Please, Your Highness," Emma whispered urgently in her ear. "This is not proper."

"I don't care, Emma. I don't care." Chloe gave her another squeeze, then held her at arm's length for a close look. "What happened? Where have you been? Who dismissed you?"

Emma glanced nervously at William.

"*He* sent you away?"

"No! I...I *thought* His Majesty did, at first." Emma offered him an apologetic smile. "I thought he was afraid of my influence over you."

Chloe thought William tried to sound innocent when he said, "Influence? I should be so lucky," but he failed miserably.

"Emma, ride with me to see my father. We need to talk. You wouldn't believe what's happened since you left."

Emma slipped out of Chloe's grasp and paced the width of the rug. "Your marriage contract is common knowledge. As is the attempt on your life in your bedchamber. Gossip has it that His Majesty brought you here to keep you safe."

"Did gossip tell you that I've been socializing with a *prime minister* for three days?"

Emma's eyebrows arched, though Chloe couldn't tell whether it was in admiration for getting through it or worry over whether she'd been successful.

"Now that you're here, would you kindly tell His

Majesty that I'm a princess, and I don't have to marry him just because he says so?''

"That's true, Your Highness—"

Chloe gloated. "Tell *him*."

Emma continued to address Chloe. "But you do have to marry him because your father says so."

KING ALBERT'S starched nurse hovered beside his bed, eyeing Chloe covertly. As if his pallor were the result of Chloe's disobedience. As if his trembling lips were due to her independent streak. As if she might do him harm.

All she wanted to do was make the old king feel better. And, if he felt better today, she wanted to convince him to void the marriage agreement.

She eased into the chair beside his bed and covered his hand, which was lying on top of the blanket, with her own. His skin was paper-thin and dry. "I'm here, Father."

Albert's eyelids fluttered. The nurse, on the other side of the bed, squinted her eyes and looked down her nose. William stood behind Chloe, his hand on her shoulder, his closeness both reassuring and distracting.

Louis sat in a chair by the window, at first physically removed from them all, until he jumped up and stalked over to the foot of the bed. "He is worse, I tell you."

His scowl was cold enough to freeze a hot ember in Hades. Chloe leaned backward, instinctively seeking William's warmth.

Louis snapped at the nurse, "Do something!"

Slowly, Albert opened his eyes halfway. His heavy-lidded gaze wavered from one face to another, around his bed, then settled on Chloe. A warm, soft smile stretched his gray lips ever so slightly. "My daughter, you are here."

"Yes, Father, I'm here." When his eyelids shuttered again, she patted his hand soothingly. "I'll just sit here awhile. You go ahead and sleep if you want to."

But Albert didn't. He opened his eyes again, wider and more focused this time, and spoke to her in a language she'd heard Moira cuss in a time or two.

Chloe needed an interpreter. "Emma—"

William leaned down by her ear. "What is wrong?"

"It...it's been too long. I can't make out everything." Chloe trusted that Emma, nearby, overheard and understood that she really meant, *What the hell is he saying?*

"Your mother," Albert wheezed in English, "was right."

If she could get him to stick to her language, she'd be okay. Emma wouldn't have to interpret. There would be less chance that someone thought Princess Moira had forgotten too much.

Chloe leaned toward the bed. "Right about what, Father?"

"She was right...to send you...to the United States."

"I enjoyed it there very much."

Off he went into his own language again.

Chloe tried to draw him back. "I enjoyed going to school there. They have wonderful colleges, Father."

"You were safe there."

"Yes, I had a fine staff who took very good care of me."

"Not like here."

Chloe frowned. "They take good care of me here,

Father. Except I want to live here in Ennsway Castle with you.''

"Not here.''

"But I belong with you, Father.''

He rambled on in his own language again. From his intense concentration and tone, Chloe sensed that whatever he was telling her was quite important. At least to him.

He closed his eyes. She patted the back of his hand gently, figuring he'd worn himself out and would sleep for hours now.

The nurse rounded the bed to Chloe's side and pushed her out of the way. In America, she might have expected such treatment in a crowd. She might have pushed back. In Ennsway, she'd already begun to get used to being treated like a princess, and getting shoved shocked her.

Out of her chair now, standing between William and the bed, Chloe looked up to see whether he was breathing fire on her behalf and fixin' to have the woman beheaded. He watched the nurse intently, his stance rigid, grasping Chloe's elbow firmly.

The nurse held Albert's wrist, then laid her fingers along the artery in his neck.

"Is he…?'' William asked.

She nodded. "He is gone.''

*Gone?*

"Do something!'' Louis shouted.

Chloe nodded vigorously in agreement.

*Moira's father just died.* How could Chloe find her to notify her?

More important to Chloe, one of the partners to the marriage contract was now dead. It was pretty obvious that he could no longer change his mind. Louis would be king now. He would inherit the obligation to enforce the contract. He would also have the power to void it if she could manage to find some way to annoy William enough to make it unanimous.

The other day, Louis had supported her. He'd agreed that she shouldn't be made to marry William. He'd help her.

Albert's secretary rushed into the room, saw for himself that His Majesty was dead. He was followed by half a dozen other men in conservative suits, one of whom placed a stethoscope to Albert's chest and listened.

Chloe finally realized no one was *doing* anything. "Aren't you going to help him?"

"His Majesty left orders not to resuscitate," Albert's secretary explained.

The doctor looked at him and nodded.

Albert's secretary, in his navy suit and striped tie, took a deep breath, pulled himself up to his full height and addressed them all, but Chloe in particular. "The King is dead. God save the queen."

*Queen?* Chloe knew Moira's mother was dead. King Albert had never remarried.

The doctor and every other nonroyal male in the room bowed in Chloe's direction. The nurse curtsied.

Emma said to Chloe, "Your Royal Majesty…"

*Majesty?*

"…if you would like to spend a short time alone with your father for a private farewell, I will clear the room."

# Chapter Eight

*I'm queen?*

"Your Majesty?"

*Of Ennsway?*

"Your Majesty."

*Of an entire country? It's mine?*

"Your Majesty!"

The last voice got her attention only because it was deep and tender and right above her ear. William.

"Uh, yes, please, I'd like a moment."

Everyone except Louis and William left the recently departed King Albert's bedchamber. Louis—she'd assumed he would be king someday, when she'd bothered to think about it at all. Moira had never told Chloe she'd inherit the throne. Surely Moira had known she was next in line. No matter that she thought it might not happen for thirty or forty years, she should have passed that tidbit of information on.

Emma would have known, too.

Everyone except Chloe, apparently. But she was supposed to be Princess Moira. She was supposed to know. She couldn't let on that she was as shocked as any American woman would be to find herself suddenly queen of an entire foreign country.

Hiding her astonishment from Louis was going to be difficult if he continued glaring at her as if he wanted her to vaporize.

"Alone," she snapped at him.

Louis paced agitatedly across the hand-sculpted carpet. He kicked a chair, sent it crashing into the wall with a splintering of dry wood. Then he left.

"Would you like me to leave, too?" William asked.

His breath teased her ear, and she couldn't think rationally. She nodded, felt his warmth withdraw and almost called him back, but she had a big problem to work through and little time in which to do it. The door shut softly behind him.

For the briefest of moments, she perched on the suede bench at the foot of the bed. She jumped to her feet, paced to the window, stared out and saw nothing, then retraced her steps and perched on the bench again.

Would Moira return to Ennsway as soon as she heard about her father's death? Was he the reason she'd dreaded coming home in the first place? Would she feel free now to expose Chloe as the impostor she really was?

The concern was fleeting; Moira wasn't the kind of person who would betray a friend. But, if the king's death precipitated any trouble, Chloe wanted to be in her own castle.

*Her* castle? Hey, everyone else thought it was hers, so it must be. Why she wanted to be there, she wasn't certain; she just knew it would make her feel better.

It was time to move home.

William would want her to return to Baesland with him, of course. She didn't know whether he really believed someone had actually tried to kill her, or whether he'd just used that as a convenient excuse to get her to Baesland where he could sway her into marrying him.

The idea of marrying him wasn't repugnant. William was a very desirable man; kind, caring, responsible, handsome, charming. She could have gone on and on. But she didn't want to marry without love.

Opening the door just far enough for his head and one shoulder, William leaned into the room. "Moira?"

At the sound of his voice, she added "tender" to the list of his good qualities.

"Would you send Emma in, please?" she asked.

Emma appeared, alone, almost instantly. "Just so you know, Your Majesty, there are others out there who think I'm not qualified to remain as your secretary because I've been out of the country too long."

"Tell them to go jump."

Emma grinned with obvious relief that Chloe wouldn't be intimidated by King Albert's incumbent staff. "I heard you snapped at your brother and ordered him out of the room."

"Yes," Chloe said smugly. "I guess I'm learning, aren't I?"

"Indeed."

"Hang on to your necklace, though. Never know when you'll have to save me from a blunder, especially now that I'm queen."

"Yes, ma'am." Emma patted her hair, too, and Chloe knew their signals were still in place, just in case.

"I guess it would be polite of me to let Louis back in now, wouldn't it?"

"It would."

"Tell him, then, and please meet me in my room in a few minutes."

"Yes, Your Majesty."

Chloe had gotten used to being called *Your Highness*. She didn't think she'd adjust quite so quickly to *Your Majesty*.

William fell into step beside her in the passageway. "We can leave for Baesland whenever you are ready."

"Ennsway is my home. I'm staying here."

"Your father would not like—"

"My father is dead."

"You are coming back with me if I have to drag you kicking and screaming the entire way."

She wheeled on him, fisted her hands on her hips and stretched up to her full height, which was a head shorter than his. "I'll have my men-at-arms throw you out if you so much as touch me."

She said a silent thank-you for having been raised with an assortment of foster brothers; they'd given her lots of practice with the peculiarities of the male of the species and how to stand up to him.

"They would not dare."

"They are *my* men-at-arms now."

"But it is not safe for you here. Did you not hear what your father said?"

For some reason, she couldn't stare him down and lie at the same time, so she resumed her path to her room. "I'm a bit rusty with the language."

"Well, I shall fill in what you missed, then. As you well know, there has never been a queen of Ennsway."

She mumbled something that she hoped sounded like agreement if he was right, and scathing if not.

"That is why your father said you were making history today." He grasped her arm and spun her around. "Moira, must I remind you? Throughout history, if the eldest child of an Ennsway king was a daughter, she never survived him.''

*He wouldn't make that up, would he?*

"You are in great danger.''

UNTIL EMMA ARRIVED, Chloe paced the hardwood floor in her sitting room. Was she in danger? Had those mishaps really been accidents? Was this why Moira's father had never brought her home until he had a prospective husband—William—in the bag? The truth about Ennsway princesses never living to become queens should have made her nervous; instead, it burned her britches.

A knock at the door received her sharp "Come in.''

"Your Majesty,'' Emma said.

"Close the door,'' Chloe ordered.

"Yes, ma'am.''

Chloe had snapped at Louis. She'd been prepared to have the men-at-arms throw William out if he'd laid a hand on her, though she would have enjoyed a little wrestling match with him first. But she'd never thought, when she'd agreed to this charade, that she'd ever have words with Emma.

"You're angry, Your Majesty?''

"You could say that.''

"Why? As queen of Ennsway, you'll have much more power than you would as princess.''

"I'm mad because William says no female has ever lived long enough to become queen!'' she shouted. "Is that reason enough? Is it even true?''

Emma stared at her feet.

Chloe's eyes narrowed at the woman she'd thought was her friend. "You knew that. You put me in danger. I guess you thought I was expendable, huh?''

Emma's head snapped up. "Oh, no—"

"Send Chloe in, let's see if she gets knocked off first," Chloe said, imitating Emma and adding a dramatic flourish.

"Your Majesty—"

Undaunted, Chloe continued, "If so, well, at least *Moira* was safe."

Emma glanced around nervously. "Please be careful what you say."

"*Be careful?* Now you want me to be careful? Why? Do you need me as a decoy a little longer?"

"Stop it!"

"Oh, I forgot. Of course you do." Her laugh was brittle. "I'm still alive."

"Let me explain!"

Chloe arched her eyebrows at Emma's lack of respect. After all, if Chloe determined that it wasn't safe to have Emma around, she had the power to banish her. Maybe worse.

"King Albert was king by accident of birth, nothing more." Emma seemed to choose her words carefully as she kept pace with Chloe across the room and back, though her path was shorter. "Likewise, *she* would have been queen by accident of birth. But you are queen because you're adventurous and unselfish."

The admiration in Emma's tone brought Chloe to a grinding halt. "*You* planned this? It was your idea?"

"Yes, Your Majesty. Out of loyalty to my country and my family, not to a spoiled princess."

This was getting interesting. Chloe didn't know whether it was true or just a good act.

"*She* would have made a poor queen, Your Majesty. If she had abdicated the throne, Louis would have made an even worse king than their father."

"Worse how?"

Emma snickered. "Oh, please! Ninety percent of the people in this country are illiterate. The hospital is no more than a place to go to die. The roads are so bad we can't attract tourists. I could go on for an hour. King Albert did nothing for the people. Louis sucks out whatever he can get his hands on. *She* wouldn't know how to correct matters, and Louis wouldn't bother."

Chloe realized she'd stopped pacing when Emma got on her soapbox. "She didn't stay in the U.S. just to avoid her father?"

"No."

"Because she might change her mind, now that he's gone. You know, have second thoughts and decide it wouldn't be so bad to be queen."

"Being queen wasn't her dream."

"People've been known to change their minds."

"Even if she did, she can't come back."

Chloe chuckled. "Why? You've got her picture posted at the border or something?"

"No, ma'am. Even if she wanted to, she could never take your place. All the records have been changed. You know, fingerprints, dental, medical…the lot."

"You can do that?"

Emma shrugged and didn't elaborate, so Chloe wasn't sure whether it was a bluff.

"I know you'll make a good queen once you get the hang of it."

"Yeah, right."

"No, I do," Emma insisted. "You have a sense of justice that I've never seen in…her."

Chloe chewed the inside of her lip. "I think you're wrong, Emma. I think she has a lot more spunk than you give her credit for. I think she'll show."

"Your Majesty…"

"Hmm?"

"If she does come for the funeral, don't think you can undo what's been done. You have no identity to return *to*."

Chloe wasn't sure, but she thought she'd just been threatened.

THE MORNING dawned bright and cheery, bringing out thousands of people. They lined up outside the curtain wall, cheering and calling out for their new queen, who presently wore jeans, sat cross-legged and barefoot in a window seat, and picked over her breakfast.

"Emma," she said, after a great deal of thought.

"I've spoken to the staff about getting you some pop-ups, Your Majesty."

Chloe hadn't even noticed what she'd been served this morning. She had bigger changes she wanted made. "Have the gates opened."

"You are going out?"

"No, I'm letting the people in."

"In, Your Majesty?"

"Yes, *in*. I like the way William does it in Baesland. People feel free to approach and talk to him. He shakes their hands and asks about their families."

"What about the danger?"

"Apparently whoever's trying to harm me—and I'm not saying anyone is—but apparently he has no difficulty getting in now. Opening the gate won't make any difference."

Emma smiled gleefully. "Then I shall tell Humphrey to get right on it."

Chloe thought Emma liked any reason to one-up

Humphrey, who, she'd confided in Chloe, had taken to her job a little too quickly when she was dismissed.

"Tradition dictates that you wave to your new subjects from the tower."

"Screw tradition."

Emma was still beaming. "Yes, I thought you might say that. Might I suggest a new location? A second-floor balcony, perhaps?"

"Sounds good. You pick it."

"I'll be most happy to. Oh, and one more thing. His Majesty, King William, has arrived and would like to see you."

Chloe set her plate down on the leather cushion and gently pushed it away with her foot. She wiggled her toes, letting the sunlight add sparkle to the pink nail polish. Yesterday had been another first for her—a pedicure. Every time she thought she was getting used to royal treatment, something else popped up.

"Send him in."

"I am already here," William, with a noticeable bounce to his step, announced on his way in.

"Your Majesty should wait to see whether Her Majesty is properly dressed," Emma scolded on her way out.

His broad smile lit up the room. "She likes me."

"She obviously wasn't too worried about you tossing her out the window for insolence."

"I reserve that only for women who refuse to marry me."

"Oh? Have there been many?"

"Just one."

Chloe abandoned the window seat, not because she was afraid he'd toss her out, but because she preferred thinking on her feet. "Did you come to invite me for a ride this morning?"

"I came to ask if you would like to choose my new apartment."

"You're tired of your old one?" If this was a trick just to get her to set foot in his castle again, so that he could lower the portcullis and keep her there, he was in for a big surprise. "Are thirty rooms too small for you?"

"No, but it is rather difficult to move them here. And I would not need anything so large."

"Here?"

"Yes, I am moving in."

"You're not invited."

"Moira, I promised your father I would protect you and marry you. If you will not come to Baesland, I shall have to come to you."

"You're not invited!"

His grin warmed his eyes. "Yes, I believe you said that already."

Repeating herself was the best she could do at the moment. Those three words said exactly what she felt. Anyone other than William would be embarrassed at having overstepped his bounds and would retreat like a hound dog with its tail between its legs.

"Your father would expect it."

His cheer was as galling as his monumental ego. "My father's dead."

"Exactly."

At a stalemate, they grew quiet enough to hear that the volume outside had risen. The crowd had drawn closer and surrounded the castle in an attempt to be heard by the queen.

William strode to the window and looked out. "How the hell did they get past the gate?"

"I ordered it opened."

"You?"

"I'm the queen, remember? I like the way you run your country. I thought I'd give it a try with mine."

*Your country, my country—what a hoot!*

For a moment, she put aside her worries. She missed Moira more than ever. She wanted to share the irony of this with her.

William's eyes twinkled again, and he casually strolled closer to her. "You like what I do?"

Was she imagining it, or was he putting more meaning into her words than a simple compliment on how he ran his monarchy?

She backed away, striving to match his casualness, but failing miserably. "I thought I'd make some changes here."

"The prime minister was right." His voice was warm and thick as he followed her slowly. "You are a breath of fresh air."

"Yeah, well, this breath of fresh air is about to go greet her subjects from a balcony."

"In jeans?"

"I suppose you think that's not proper for a queen? That I should wear an expensive dress and don a crown?"

"Yes, but I will marry you anyway."

She turned and took a couple steps toward the door, but decided she'd rather keep her eye on him and resumed her backward retreat.

"It is not safe for you to go outside," he cautioned.

"How can you say that? You have people wandering through your castle."

"No one has reason to want me dead."

"Don't push your luck."

"I have never heard that expression before."

"It means—"

"Oh, do not worry, Moira. I know what it means. I can tell just from the fire in your eyes."

"I don't have fire—"

"And the blush on your cheeks."

Her back bumped up against a wall. "Stop that."

He closed the gap until they were toe-to-toe, his head towering above hers as he held her with nothing more than the heat in his eyes. "And the way the tiny pulse in your neck beats faster."

She hadn't realized until that moment that he hadn't done his ritual cheek-kissing thing this morning. As he dipped his head toward her, she told herself that was all he was doing. As she felt his warm breath caress her cheek, she wished for him to get it over with before she grabbed him and showed him how an American woman kissed.

As his lips touched hers, her eyelids fluttered shut and her heart pounded so hard she was sure he could hear it.

"Moira," he whispered against her lips. "I have wanted to do this since I first saw you on the plane."

As his lips closed over hers again, as he tasted them from one corner to the other, her fingers reached for something safe, something other than him to hold—anything—lest she crush herself against him.

Her hand hit something hard, knocked it to the floor where it crashed and splintered. Shards bit into the top of her foot and her toes.

His broad chest brushed against her breasts as he

turned and stared down at hundreds of colorful chunks littering the floor. Her gaze followed his.

"I trust you were not going to hit me over the head with that?"

"No, I…I bumped it. With my hand."

His palms slid down her arms until her fingers were engulfed by his. "Perhaps the antiques would be safer if your hands were better occupied."

"Antiques? Oh, God. Oh, God." She broke loose from his grasp and stared down at the vase. "What did I break?"

"Nothing that can be replaced, I am sure."

It looked old, what she could see of the fragments and chunks scattered around. Really, really old. "It's Egyptian, isn't it?"

"Yes, I should think so."

As if she were a child who'd touched a no-no and broken it, she thought somebody was going to be very mad. Careless of her knees, she knelt down amid the remains. "Oh, God, they'll kill me."

"Who?"

"The…uh…" But everything in the castle was hers, wasn't it? All the same, she'd had enough education to feel bad about the piece of ancient history she'd just destroyed. "The maids."

"They will clean it up without a word." He crouched beside her. "Leave it."

She picked up two jagged pieces and butted them together. "Maybe it can be glued." No matter what angle she tried, they didn't match up.

Careful not to cut her, he wrenched the shards from her fingers and dropped them amid the others on the floor. "If it can be repaired, there are others who will tend to it."

He was dangerously close, his hands on hers, their shoulders brushing.

She popped to her feet, like a piece of bread in a toaster escaping the heat before it burned. "Gotta go."

"Your feet are bare."

"My maid'll get me some shoes."

The room spun for a brief moment as she found herself scooped up in his arms, held snugly against his chest.

"I would not want you to cut your feet," he explained.

"Put me down." It should have sounded like a command, but even Chloe had to admit it wasn't much stronger than a whisper.

"I think I shall." He stepped clear of the debris, but still held her so close she could feel his heart beating against her ribs. "If you will call me by my name."

*William.* She'd be lost if she said it out loud. She was nearly lost just hearing it in her head.

"Okay. Put me down, Bill." It was so ludicrous a name for him that she burst out laughing.

He dumped her to her feet. "Who is this Bill?"

"It's a nickname for William."

"Will is a nickname. Bill is...is... If your father were not already dead, I think I would kill him for sending you to live in a country that butchers a man's name into a duck's anatomy."

Chloe spotted Angela lurking just outside the doorway. "Angela, I need a pair of shoes before I go outside to meet the people."

"Yes, ma'am." Angela rushed away.

"You told the prime minister that you were not partial to tradition. How did you put it?" William grinned. "Ah, yes, I remember. 'Royal brouhaha.'"

"That's true."

"Yet it is tradition for the new sovereign to greet the people."

"Well, I'm in jeans. I won't wear a crown or anything."

"It is still tradition."

"And I'll give 'em a real wave, not one of those dinky little royal wrist rotations."

"No, I must object."

"Tough toenails."

"Damn your American influence!" William ranted.

"I hear it's just what this country needs."

CHLOE SLIPPED into the flats Angela had brought her, along with a denim jacket to match her jeans. If the people wanted American influence, American influence they would get.

Angela beamed. "You look like...model."

As Chloe approached the doorway to the balcony Emma had selected, the crowd's chanting grew louder and more distinct. It sounded as if hundreds of people were partying out in the bailey. Celebrating.

As she stepped out onto the balcony, a collective roar went up. The force of it nearly shoved her backward into the castle.

"Smile." How she heard Emma's advice, she had no idea.

"I didn't know there were so many people out here." Not hundreds, but thousands.

"You're doing fine. Now wave."

Simple instructions, but difficult to follow at first. Chloe had never stood in front of thousands of people for anything, much less a crowd that cheered her every movement, the least little smile, the raising of her hand above the stone railing.

Surprisingly, she was not unaware of what William was up to—maybe because, since she knew so few people in Ennsway, he represented an anchor in her life. Just before she stepped outside, he'd grabbed the nearest man-at-arms, barked at him and scowled at others, and now he had several stationed around nearby windows and doors.

She watched the Ennswayans below; the men-at-arms scrutinized them. All she saw were happy, smiling, laughing people who were pleased to have a new ruler. Pleased that it was she.

When Emma said, "That's better," Chloe took stock and discovered that her smile had grown and her wave was genuine. She was truly enjoying herself. Who wouldn't want to be loved by thousands?

William stood behind her. Oh, he was out of sight of the crowd. He hovered just inside the doorway, several feet back, but she could feel him anyway. She knew he watched her every movement, protectively, because he believed she was in danger. After that kiss they'd shared, *she* suspected he might seize the first opportunity to pounce on her and gleefully claim he was coming to her defense.

She remained unconvinced that she was in danger. These people obviously meant her no harm, and she would not take to hiding inside stone walls just to pacify William.

If he didn't like her going out among the people alone, let him come with her. There was work to be done in Ennsway, and, for these wonderful people who welcomed her with open arms, she was fixin' to give her best.

CHLOE SAT in the huge leather chair behind King Albert's centuries-old desk. She'd never studied antique furniture; it wasn't something that had interested her. Now she regretted it. Such history! Perhaps wars had been declared across its surface. Perhaps treaties had been penned on it by candlelight.

King Albert's secretary interrupted Chloe's musings. "Your Majesty..."

Perhaps she should get her mind back on the business at hand.

The desktop was covered with telegrams, cards, notes, and letters. Some were in English, some were not. Some spoke of sympathy, others requested that they not be forgotten by the new sovereign.

"Here are the reports on the farms, the forests, the marina." He dropped several heavy journals on the desk with a thunk. "And the gamekeeper's report, the dairy report, the family's personal financial report..."

Chloe thought her head would burst. Nothing she had ever done had prepared her to run a country. What had Emma and Moira been thinking when they talked her into this? Chloe liked college science courses, field trips, hours spent in a lab. She'd declined every business class ever offered. She hadn't taken speed-reading, which was what she'd need if she was to finish all these thick reports by her hundredth birthday.

"Before you do all that, Your Majesty," Emma interjected, "there are some decisions for you to make on your father's funeral."

"Decisions?" King Albert's secretary asked in horror. "What decisions? There are no decisions!"

"We'll leave that up to Her Majesty, now won't we?" Emma said firmly.

"No, we will not!"

"There is the matter of a death tax," Emma stated to Chloe. "You remember, upon the king's death, all subjects are taxed."

Chloe compared the opulence of the spacious office, large enough to hold a ball in, to the people who wore patches on their clothes, had no school system to speak of, whose roads were in disrepair, and whose hospital was a place to go to die. "And what is the tax used for?"

"To pay for everything from the burial robe, the casket, the flowers, the procession—"

Chloe picked up the financial report. She'd never had accounting, either, but her own checkbook ledger didn't have enough columns to allow such large numbers. Nobody's did. "The family will pay for my father's funeral."

"But, Your Majesty, I must object!"

"Very good," Emma said at the same time.

Chloe looked at her father's secretary. "Leave us." When she noticed Emma patting her hair, Chloe knew she was in safe territory. "I'll send for you if I need you."

"Yes, Your Majesty, though I do so with the greatest reservation—"

"Uh-huh." Chloe waited for the door to close behind him. "What else, Emma?"

"There are people who want an audience with you, Your Majesty."

"Such as?"

"The head of nearly every family, for starters. Then there are phone calls to return to Queen Elizabeth, President Clinton—"

"You've got to be kidding."

"I never kid, Your Majesty. You should also look

through your mail and draft a few replies which will guide me in how I am to answer the rest of your correspondence. You know, use a dash of your American colloquialism. It's so charming.''

"Boy, have you changed your tune."

Emma acknowledged Chloe's point with a graceful smile.

Chloe took a deep breath, scooted her chair closer to the desk and asked, "Where should I start?"

"How about seeing a few of your visitors?"

"You'll be here, too, right? Patting your hair and playing with your necklace and all that?"

"Yes, Your Majesty."

Besides her signals, Emma had to translate. After the first visitor, Chloe wrote down a few words in the Ennswayan language and kept them on her desk, so that she could at least say "Welcome" and "Thank you for coming."

When Emma announced a lunch break hours later, Chloe slumped in the huge chair, slithered out toward the edge of the seat and onto the floor like a limp noodle.

"What are you doing?" Emma asked with some concern.

"As soon as I recover, I'm going to stretch out these kinks."

"There is no time for that."

"There has to be."

The morning's duties had been nearly as stressful as dealing with a broken washing machine, changing the oil in her jeep and standing in the wrong checkout line anywhere. But she could yell at the landlord, she could sometimes con a nice young man into thinking it a privilege to work on an antique jeep, and the longest she'd ever stood in line was twenty minutes.

Beneath the desk, Chloe saw a man approach, wearing dark pants and black shoes.

"Get rid of him," she ordered Emma. She didn't want to see anyone else for a month. "Tell him to come back this afternoon."

"What the devil?" William demanded.

Chloe's first impulse was to dash to her feet, but her aching back and stiff neck objected enough that she remembered she had every right to be lying on her back on the floor behind her father's desk.

No…behind *her* desk.

William dashed around the corner and crouched beside her. He touched her arm with the same concern he had had after her fall from the horse. "What has happened?"

"I've inherited a small country, that's what's happened." With her free hand, she rubbed one temple in small circles. There was no way she was going to raise her other arm and deprive it of William's touch.

"Is that all?"

"There are a million decisions to make, a ton of reports to read—"

"Hundreds of people waiting outside to speak to you. Yes, I know, Moira."

"Say that again."

"There are hundreds of people—"

"No, my name."

"You want me to say your name?"

"Yes."

"I thought I was to style you as 'Your Majesty.'"

"Ah, but you slipped, didn't you?"

"I shall be more careful."

"Please don't."

"Does this mean you will marry me soon?"

"It means, simply, that I'm exhausted, and I like the way you say 'Moira.'"

"You do?"

"Say it."

"I will say it if you will call me William again."

"Okay."

"And never that other name, that duck part."

She giggled, grateful for his light mood. "Thank you, William."

"It is my pleasure, Moira. Now, we should go."

"Where?"

"Wherever you like. Food, fresh air, change of scenery—you name it."

"But there are hundreds of people outside that door."

"There are private passages, Moira. Surely you have not forgotten their existence."

"Oh. No, of course not. Lead the way."

He rose in one smooth motion and held his hand down for her. She slipped hers into his firm grasp and let him help her to her feet. Suddenly her back didn't ache so much, her neck was limber again, and she was hungry, but not tired.

He led her through a door that looked exactly like every other panel in the wall, except that it had a door-knob. In the brick passage, he turned immediately right, then chose the downstairs route.

"You certainly know your way around my castle," Chloe said.

"I know my way around being a monarch, too, Moira. I will be your friend and help you acclimate to the job, if you like."

Taking his hand was as natural as breathing, and Chloe let it serve as her answer as he led her out onto the wallwalk, where she was required to do no more than nod at a person below from time to time. And a good thing, too, because her mind wandered more along the lines of what it would be like to marry William, to walk by his side in daylight, and sleep by his side at night.

"What are you thinking?" he asked after a while.

She couldn't tell him the truth about *that*. "They don't look sad until they see me," she said instead.

"They may not have liked Albert, but they know he was your father. Now, if you have had enough fresh air, it would do you good to eat."

She nodded, and he took her hand from his and tucked it into the crook of his elbow as they made their way back inside the castle. There, when the occasional person made as if to approach and speak to her, he quickly took note of William's protective glare, bowed his head respectfully to Chloe and changed direction.

Amused, she said, "You don't have to do that, you know."

"What?"

"Scare everyone away."

"I do not know what you mean."

She could tell by his tone that he did. "Thanks, William."

CHLOE HID OUT in her sitting room as long as she dared the next morning. She'd made enough decisions in the past couple days to last a lifetime. She needed some time to herself where no one would ask anything of her.

Everyone thought she was burying her father today,

when, in fact, she'd met the man only a handful of times. They weren't really related, and she'd hardly known him, though she would've liked to have had more time and gotten to know him better.

In truth, she wasn't burying her father, but her past. She was in charge now, and it was time for her to take control of her future as queen of Ennsway, and only Ennsway. Not Baesland. She would have to tell William.

Emma opened the door soundlessly and glided in. "*She's* here, Your Majesty."

The emphasis on *she* told Chloe exactly who Emma meant. "I knew she'd show."

"You sound as if you're proud of her."

"I am. Scared to death, but proud. She's never traveled on her own before. Heck, she's never done anything on her own before. Well—" Chloe grinned "—except for that time or two when we, uh, you know."

"You want to see her, then?"

"Emma, she's been my best friend for ten years."

Emma glanced at her wristwatch. "The funeral procession—"

"Bring her to me."

"Yes, Your Majesty."

While Emma went for Moira, Chloe got ten minutes to wonder what was running through Moira's mind. Was Ennsway as she remembered it? Was she at her wit's end, traveling on her own? She was here in time for the funeral—would she hate the lack of tradition, the downplaying of the brouhaha that Chloe had ordered?

Now that there was a marriage contract, would Moira want William when she saw him? The thought gave Chloe a shiver as she suddenly, briefly, saw a future without William in it.

The door to the suite opened. One look at her friend, and Chloe and Moira were in each other's arms for a tight hug.

"God, I missed you!" Moira said, then sniffed.

"I never thought this would be so hard," they said in unison, then laughed about it.

"I'm sorry about your father," Chloe said. "Did you know he was ill?"

Moira shook her head. "Emma and I were grossly underinformed of everything. So, how's it feel to be queen?"

Chloe stepped back. "How's it feel *not* to be queen?"

"Terrific!"

Chloe didn't realize she'd been holding her breath until she heard Moira's answer. "You know about the marriage contract?"

"Yes, Emma's told me everything."

Chloe whispered, just in case someone could hear, "Do you regret giving this up?"

"And having to marry King William? No way." She studied Chloe for all of one second and laughed. "Careful, your eyes are going to pop right out of your head."

"I can't believe you said that about marrying William."

"Oh?" Moira teased as she slowly circled around Chloe. "It's 'William,' is it?"

"Well..."

"You like him, huh?"

*Like?* "Oh, yeah."

"Have you seen his castle yet?"

"Mmm-hmm."

"That's some damned fortress, isn't it?"

Chloe was surprised how much Moira's opinion of William's home differed from her own, but, at the same time, it relieved her mind about Moira wanting to take her country back. And William. "I liked it."

"Good. Then I guess you're wondering why I'm here."

"I assume you came for the funeral."

"Right. Could you arrange a few minutes for me alone with my father? I have a few things I need to say to him."

"Hey, I'm queen, remember? I can do anything."

Moira grinned. "Don't get too cocky." She reached into her purse and pulled out a photograph. "I brought you a picture of your dog. I thought you might be worried about her."

Chloe accepted it and held it next to her heart for a moment, then laughed.

"What's so funny?"

"I was thinking about how Friday would've treated William if I'd brought her here. How is she?"

"She misses you. She sticks close to me, but she won't let me touch her. Now that you're in charge, you want me to send her to you?"

Chloe weighed the joy she would feel in having Friday back against the dog making the long trip alone in a crate, not knowing where she'd end up or when. "Let me think about it."

"Okay." Moira pulled out a piece of paper and handed it to Chloe. "I got a job," she said proudly. "That's the address where I'll be this summer. It's a dude ranch, and I'm the riding instructor."

"Uh, you do know, don't you, that you'll be teaching them to ride western?"

"Of course. I'm no dummy. And, thanks to losing a few bets with you over the years, I learned more about it than those dudes are likely to know."

"You need to impress the boss, not the dudes."

"Oh! You want to see his picture?" Moira rummaged through her purse as if she'd carried one her whole adult life. "It's in the brochure."

Chloe stared at the picture of the rugged cowboy and knew Moira was in way over her head. This guy would be able to tack a horse on the darkest night, probably learned to ride before he learned to walk and would see right through her.

"Handsome, isn't he?" Moira asked. "In a rugged sort of way."

"Well, he doesn't hold a candle to William, of course," she teased.

"I always thought he was a pompous ass."

"He must've outgrown it."

Just as they were talking about him, he appeared at the door, behind Emma.

"His Majesty has arrived to escort you, Your Majesty," Emma said. "If you're ready?"

"Almost. Moi—my friend Chloe will go with you, Emma. She asked a favor, and I'd like you to arrange it immediately. I'll wait here with His Majesty until it's taken care of."

"Yes, Your Majesty."

"Thanks," Moira said as she engulfed Chloe in their last hug. "Write me, okay?"

"Oh, yeah, that'll look good at the dude ranch."

"Oh, one more thing." Moira reached into her purse and, without rooting around this time, pulled out a box of pop-ups and tossed them to Chloe. "Emma said you were dying for these."

Chloe caught it neatly, greedily. "Yum, strawberry. My favorite."

"Of course. What're friends for?"

When the door closed behind Emma and Moira, William said, "You and your friend are very close."

"Yes."

"You look very much alike."

*Did he suspect?* "You think?"

"You could be sisters."

*No, of course not.*

"I always wanted a sister."

"We will have to be sure our first child has a sister."

"William…"

"Perhaps it is too soon after your father's death to discuss this."

"As a matter of fact, this is as good a time as any. Now that I'm queen, William, I'm calling off the wedding."

"But there is a contract."

"You can't enforce it."

He stepped forward and brushed the back of his hand softly across her cheek. "You are distraught."

*Oh, puh-lease.* "I am entirely coherent." Coherent enough to know she wanted his love.

"We will discuss this again after you have had time to adjust to your loss."

She allowed him to pull her hand into the crook of his elbow and escort her out the door. "I won't change my mind."

"We shall see."

offer, Ung and tossed it off to Chloe. "Damn sure you need it this time."

Chloe knew it was a mistake. "Thanks, Andrew."

My turn?

"OK to me. What's the big deal?"

When the house had cooled down considerably, William said, "Tell me, my friend, are you a . . . Chloe?"

# Chapter Nine

When Chloe and Moira had agreed to trade places, Chloe had planned on the freedom to indulge her first loves—studying and learning—by taking some college courses in Europe, but it was obvious that there were several reasons why furthering her education would have to wait. While a princess might get into a car and drive off to a nearby country for a week of classes, she didn't think it was going to be so easy to convince anyone that a reigning queen could commute. Travel was a problem in Ennsway, also, unless she was willing to major in pothole evasion. And her desktop was still covered with reports that she really needed to peruse.

In the meantime, she found the atrium as close to a field trip as she was likely to get. Armed with books from the castle's library, she ate breakfast in the sun-warmed room each morning and read up on native flora. She also had French-English and German-English dictionaries at hand, as only one of the books was in English. It was almost heaven.

And it just got better when a small lizard scurried across her table, down an iron leg and across the cobblestone floor. Chloe dashed back to the library for a book on fauna to help her identify her visitor. She made only one wrong turn in the whole round trip.

William sat directly across from her, a health-care journal open and ignored on the round tabletop in front of him. He sipped his coffee and watched Chloe with an amused expression. "You certainly acquired a thirst for knowledge while you were in the United States."

"Can't have too much knowledge," she mumbled as she read, her breakfast completely forgotten.

Humphrey entered the atrium. "Excuse me, Your Majesty." When both William and Chloe looked up at him, he clarified with "Ma'am. There is a child who says you asked her to visit you." Chloe thought she must have looked stumped, because he enlightened her with "She has brought a puppy with her."

"Oh, the little redhead from the day I arrived? The one who was afraid I'd take her puppy away?" Humphrey looked at her blankly, but Chloe knew she was correct. "Bring her in."

"Your breakfast is getting cold," William cautioned.

Chloe still hadn't gotten used to his presence, even though he'd shadowed her all week, still insisting he had to fulfill his promise to her father and keep her safe.

Now, instead of blaring her stereo to make him send her away, as she had in Baesland Castle, she lay in bed in the morning trying to think of ways to make him want her for herself. Of course, she knew that the only way to find a man really right for her was to *be* herself, the way William was himself.

And she liked everything she saw—in spite of his apparent amusement, he was interested enough to pull the reptile book over to his side of the table and study it—except his determination to marry her whether she liked it or not.

"Hello, Your Royal Majesty."

Chloe turned in her chair and saw the adorable little red-haired girl, whose arms overflowed with a bright-eyed black spaniel puppy. About halfway down into a curtsy, she lost her balance, and the puppy scrambled free.

"You speak English," Chloe said with surprise.

"Little bit, Your Majesty," her mother said from the doorway. She smiled shyly and executed a perfect curtsy.

At least it was perfect by royal standards. By Chloe's, it was the silliest she'd seen yet. It made her wonder which had come first—curtsying or genuflecting? And had it been out of respect or to serve some egomaniac?

Chloe waved the mother forward, and she in turn sent her daughter chasing after the puppy until she caught it. "She wanted...to speak to you, so...I teach her...little bit. You understand?"

Chloe smiled. "Yes, I understand you fine. What's your name?"

"I am Hilda. My daughter is Anna."

"Hey, Anna, let me see your puppy," Chloe said, and when she got it, she let it wriggle on her lap and lick her chin.

Anna giggled by Chloe's knee.

Hilda frowned, wrung her hands and fidgeted from one foot to the other. "You are not afraid, Your Majesty?"

"No, of course not. Why would I be?"

"I know you are afraid of dogs."

*I am?*

Moira had been afraid of Friday. Now that Chloe thought about it, she'd never seen Moira pet a dog in the entire time she'd known her. "This is just a pup, Hilda. And besides, I like dogs."

"Her Majesty was very attached to her friend's dog in the United States," William related, "and it was quite a nasty thing."

Chloe couldn't believe he'd noticed. "Friday?"

"That disagreeable animal growled at me the entire time it was in my car."

"Oh." Chloe remembered telling Emma she'd hoped Friday didn't bite William's trousers, and hoped she wasn't blushing now at the thought. She hadn't given a fig for his suit. It was what was in the suit that she'd liked. And still did.

William crooked his index finger, and Anna shyly moved to his side. Her shyness disappeared when he showed her the picture of the lizard and spoke to her in her own language. She leaned on his chair and looked up as he pointed at the tree it had climbed.

Already twenty-eight, Chloe knew she wanted children someday. She'd never gone so far as to picture her future babies, but suddenly she saw raven-haired, lapis-eyed children toddling around on the cobblestone floor, chasing a lizard. William would help them catch it, and she would show them how to identify it, then release it. Might as well put all that education to use somewhere.

If only he could love her, not feel obligated to marry her because he'd promised her father he'd protect her.

"Come, Anna," Hilda said. "I go work now."

"Do you work here, Hilda?"

"Yes, Your Majesty, in the kitchen. Anna is good."

Hilda sounded as though she were trying to reassure her queen. "No trouble."

"Does she come with you every day?"

"No! Today only. My sister sick today."

Chloe figured that meant no baby-sitter. "Let her stay in the atrium awhile. The puppy can't hurt anything in here."

Hilda looked uncertain.

"I'll have Humphrey bring her to you when I finish my breakfast."

Hilda frowned at the unfinished food on Chloe's plate. "You no like?"

With a wave of her hand at the table, Chloe indicated the books lying open there. "I saw a lizard."

"You afraid of lizard?"

Chloe laughed. "No, I wanted to see what kind it is."

Hilda looked quite skeptical that anyone would pass up a good hot breakfast for pictures in a book. Anna spoke, and her mother translated, her eyes beaming now. "Anna wants to know when you get married."

"Oh..."

"Soon," William answered over his coffee cup. "Very soon."

Hilda's nervousness disappeared, and she became quite animated. "The wedding...will be so beautiful. All the womans know it is better when you marry. Our children...will go to school. Our husbands...will work to fix the roads."

Chloe was confused, and not by Hilda's halting English. "They can do that if I don't marry."

"No, you must marry His Majesty."

"Yes," he agreed with an amused grin, "you must."

Chloe kicked him under the table, but since she'd kicked off her shoes and was in her sock feet, he didn't even acknowledge it.

"His Majesty...will make Ennsway much better place to live. And he...will have more farmland. Ennsway farmland is good. Is good dowry."

Chloe looked at William and got a creepy feeling in the pit of her stomach. "You want to marry me for farmland?" She was glad she hadn't eaten much breakfast. "My father signed me away like...like a bushel of corn?"

Hilda continued as if Chloe's accusation had gone over her head, which it probably had. "Your Majesty, please, I ask question?" she asked William.

"Yes, Hilda." He seemed quite unruffled by Chloe's rising temper.

"Is true, you put man in dungeon to protect Her Majesty?"

Chloe glared at him. "You didn't!"

Hilda, beaming, clasped her hands together over her heart. "So romantic!"

"Yes, I did, Hilda." Through his smile, he muttered, "Thank you very much."

"That's barbaric," Chloe snapped.

He shrugged.

"It's archaic!"

Hilda frowned and fidgeted from one foot to the other, then apparently decided the atrium was not the place to be at the moment. "Anna, come!" She grabbed her daughter and the puppy and left Their Majesties to duke it out.

"Excuse me, but this is the twentieth century," Chloe pointed out to William. "Nearly the twenty-first. You can't have me because you signed a piece of paper, and you can't throw men in the dungeon because...because... Why *did* you?"

"He was responsible for your mare once she was saddled. He left his post."

Chloe slammed a book shut. "I'd hate to think what you'd do with a man if he actually committed a crime."

"I rather like the old way, myself. If a man steals, cut off his hand."

Only the twinkle in his eyes gave him away, or Chloe would have taken off for the United States without waiting for a plane. "I want to see him."

"Why?"

"A dungeon is cold and damp and filled with torture things."

He shrugged. "Maybe not so damp."

OUTSIDE THE ATRIUM, Prince Louis intercepted Hilda, Anna, and the puppy. "What the devil is that dog doing in the castle?"

Hilda urged Anna to keep moving toward the kitchen, and she carefully kept herself between the child and Louis.

"Dogs have not been allowed in Ennsway for more than fifteen years, by His Majesty's orders." King Albert's law had not been strictly enforced for quite some time, especially on the smaller breeds. "Certainly not in the castle."

"Her Majesty, she ask to see it."

"Never!"

"Is true, Your Highness. You ask her."

"Stop right there."

Hilda stopped as ordered, but, at a quiet word from

her mother, Anna disappeared around the nearest corner and hugged her puppy tightly.

"Her Majesty asked to see that puppy?"

Hilda nodded vigorously. "Yes."

"She wasn't afraid of it?"

"No."

"Not even the teensiest bit frightened?"

Hilda shook her head and repeated Chloe's explanation. "Is only a puppy."

Louis smoothed his beard with his fingers. "Hmm, yes, so it was. Very interesting." And, without dismissing Hilda, he walked away, deep in thought. "Very interesting, indeed."

AT BAESLAND CASTLE, the limo crossed the moat bridge and drew to a stop at the inner gatehouse. William quickly motioned the driver away and held out his own hand to help Moira out of the car. For a moment, he thought she would refuse his assistance, but then she slipped her fingers into his palm, and he nearly forgot they were there to inspect the dungeon.

He had better places he would like to inspect with her. Like his bedroom. He had been a guest at her castle for a week. He had dined with her, ridden with her, pretended to read the newspaper in the same room with her. He had held her chair, inhaled hints of the exotic coconut perfume she favored and nearly gone out of his mind wanting her.

Out of respect for the recent loss of her father, he had been a perfect gentleman. Well, he was done with that; he would take a chance.

"You are sure you want to see the dungeon?"

She tilted her head up at him and, with a sly smile, asked, "Is there some reason you don't want me to?"

"You have never visited my apartment." He hoped his grin was not a leer.

"Do you keep prisoners there, too?"

"No, Moira, I do not."

"Women who have refused to marry you, perhaps?"

Momentarily beaten, he sighed and motioned for her to follow him through a low doorway and down the narrow, winding steps to the dungeon. He would have let her precede him, but it was not the best footing for a lady. Even if the lady wore running shoes and jeans.

The dimly lit area smelled musty, he noted with some dismay. Not that that was a bad thing in a dungeon, but she would undoubtedly hold it against him.

What he really wanted her to hold against him was herself. If he could get her in and out of the dungeon, then off somewhere alone, perhaps he could restore the camaraderie they had shared over breakfast in the atrium.

If he had known she liked lizards and such, he would have taken it upon himself to get her outdoors more often. He would have taken her for a walk instead of a ride, and he would have been able to hold her hand.

She had spent two hours poring over books on native trees and plants. Perhaps she would like the view from the mountaintop that soared another mile above Baesland Castle. He could have the driver take them up there—

Her nose wrinkled. "It's filthy."

He glanced around at the rough-cut floors and walls, the low ceiling which made him stoop. "It is a dungeon." And she had only seen the outer chamber.

"Where is he?"

William turned to the man who had been unlucky

enough to draw guard duty today. "Her Majesty would like to see the prisoner."

"Yes, Your Majesty."

William followed him through another short, narrow doorway to the torture chamber. The most prominent apparatus in the room was the Roman rack in the center. He dared not turn and see Moira's reaction. He did not want to see the loathing in her eyes.

It was only a few short steps to the row of cells. To himself, William swore that this dungeon used to be larger than it appeared now; he would never admit to Moira that it had been too long since he saw it. She lingered a moment by the rack, then followed him, and her critical presence made him aware that centuries of little use had done nothing to eliminate an underlying pervasion of body odors.

"It smells worse than a pig farm in July."

Idly he wondered when she had ever set foot within fifty miles of a pig farm. In any month.

THREE POORLY LIT CELLS backed up against the outer wall. The prisoner slumped on the floor, his back against the side bars of the middle cell.

"It's wet."

"Most dungeons are damp."

"Damp? I can hear water trickling in."

"It is the moat."

The prisoner jumped to his feet, bumped his head on the ceiling with a solid thunk and ducked, his hand pressed to the top of his head.

"Are they treating you well?" Moira asked him.

"Yes, ma'am."

She looked doubtful.

"I think Her Majesty wants to know if we have subjected you to any torture devices," William hinted.

The prisoner looked suitably shocked. "Oh, no, ma'am. Just the low ceiling."

"What is your name?"

"Patrick, Your Majesty."

Moira pivoted in a slow circle, taking in her surroundings. While she did that, William blessed the low lighting that prevented her seeing all, and cursed the low lighting that equally prevented him enjoying her full circle. She had a delightful body, kept in athletic shape from the riding she did and the exercise routine he suspected she still practiced each day. Though he was beginning to doubt he would ever see her in that cropped sweatshirt again until after they were wed.

She turned up her nose and squared off with William. "When is his trial?"

"I am still looking into the matter of your accident."

"So you *do* think it was an accident!"

"I was being sarcastic."

Patrick rubbed his head where he had bumped it. "I admit I left my post, Your Majesty," he said to Moira. "It was only for a minute to help your secretary, but I did it, and it was wrong. But I would never harm you, ma'am, you must believe me."

"Silence!" his guard hissed.

"I have family in Ennsway. Uncles and cousins and such. They want our countries united as much as we do here in Baesland."

The guard tore a club from the wall and rapped on the bars of the cell in warning.

"Stop that," Moira snapped at him.

William was caught in a quandary. Did he side with his man-at-arms and tell Patrick to shut the hell up, or did he side with Moira, be compassionate and earn points?

"William, make him stop."

A nod of his head, and the guard backed off.

"We all want the wedding soon, ma'am, so as to benefit everyone in both countries. New farm equipment, fresh food, new jobs, education—my family wants this, and so do I. We've been preparing for the event since we heard His Majesty asked for your hand."

William thought the man sounded like a walking advertisement, which, under other circumstances, would have been an admirable thing.

"Let him go," Moira ordered.

"You cannot believe he meant you no harm."

"He sounds sincere."

"Yes." William turned and addressed Patrick, "Remind me to recommend you to the theater guild when you are released."

*In a hundred years.*

"Well?" Moira tapped her toe on the stone floor. It made little noise, but William did not miss her meaning.

He faced her again and waited. If this was the only way he was going to get to see any of her passion, he was not about to miss a second of it.

"I could never marry a man who keeps another in such deplorable conditions."

He sighed. "Guard, release the prisoner."

"Yes, Your Majesty."

The guard fumbled for the proper key. Moira headed for the exit.

William lingered behind, knowing he could not let this excuse for a man go free. Moira's life might mean nothing to her, but he could not bear the thought of any harm coming to her.

As an aside, he whispered to the guard, "Lock him in the tower instead."

WILLIAM PACED his dressing room. "Damn it, Leonard, if I keep on at this rate, the three months are going to be up. I thought Her Majesty would at least like to pick her wedding date."

"Does she know she has a deadline?"

He raked his fingers through his hair, aware that it was becoming a most annoying habit. "You mean, has she read the contract? Probably backward and forward, looking for a loophole." He glanced in the full-length mirror. "Am I so repulsive?"

"If the constant marriage proposals that come in your mail are any indication, I think not."

He turned sideways and checked his reflection to see whether he had developed a gut overnight. "There, see, I keep in shape."

"Of course you do."

"I dress well."

"Most definitely."

"I am also kind to small children."

Speaking of small children brought the red-haired Anna to mind, the way she had tried to hold on to her puppy while she curtsied to them in the atrium, the musical lilt of her giggles as she'd stood at Moira's knee. Moira had been patient with her, entranced by her, generous in her offer to let her stay and play while her mother worked. A most unusual queen. She would make a wonderful mother to his children.

If he ever got that close.

He wanted children, not just because he needed an

heir, but because he liked them, and they were the future. He wanted half a dozen, but he could compromise one way or the other, depending on what Moira wanted.

"I do not wish to wait until the deadline, Leonard."

"They have been working day and night on Her Majesty's gown. Everyone in Baesland and Ennsway is ready to pull together at a moment's notice. I daresay you could have the wedding soon."

"Then I shall tell her today that we will wait no longer."

Leonard's face fell in dismay, but he quickly resumed his perpetual unruffled mask. "Might I make a suggestion, Your Majesty?"

His secretary was not a yes-man, and so William nodded for him to proceed, though he thought he was about to get a repeat of Leonard's earlier advice.

"Perhaps if you would…romance Her Majesty?"

William folded his arms across his chest and waited for him to continue.

"Women, sir, if I may say so, do not take kindly to being bulldozed into matters such as these."

"Bulldozed? I have been most patient with her."

"You are a king, used to getting your way, if I might say so, sir. She is a queen, used to getting her way. Women sometimes need a gentle hand. Soft music. Candlelight. Flowers."

William renewed his pacing. "I have never done this before." He had never had to. Women lined up outside his door, both marriageable ones and ones with marriage-minded daughters. Others proposed by mail. Last time he had danced at Buckingham Palace, he had had half a dozen propositions whispered in his ear before ten o'clock. "I would not know how."

"Welcome to the real world," Leonard mumbled.

"What?"

"I said, women make it a confusing world, Your Majesty."

"I have learned how to please a woman, how to sidestep a woman, but...romance one? How do I do this?"

"Tell her she is beautiful."

"She is."

"But have you told her?"

"I am sure she knows it."

Leonard sighed. "You must tell her."

"I must? Then I shall."

"You must treat her special, like no one else does."

"Everyone treats her special."

"Yes, I know. You have your work cut out for you there, I'm afraid. She's used to the very best. The Andalusian mare was a good start."

William frowned. "She told me to take her back."

"Yes, but you didn't, and she still rides her, doesn't she?"

He nodded, deep in thought about what Moira liked. "She likes to study, to read books. She was absolutely delighted to watch a lizard the other morning."

"You shouldn't give her a lizard, Your Majesty."

He scowled at Leonard. "Do not mock me."

"Never, Your Majesty."

"I had thought about taking her up the mountain to see the view. She likes trees, and there are deer up there."

"Wow," Leonard mumbled.

"What?"

"I said, the road will need to be plowed if you intend to take her up to the snowcap."

"Yes." He felt renewed energy in his step. "Yes, I believe she will find that romantic. Leonard, have a hot meal planned at the summit. And a windscreen."

"I'll have everything in order. All you have to do is be charming and romantic."

"I can do that."

"YOU LOOK quite beautiful today," William told Moira as he helped her into the limo.

She misstepped and bumped her head.

He scooted in beside her and patted her head soothingly, allowing the motion to change gradually into stroking her silky hair. He was glad she no longer knotted it into that skull-hugging braid. It was so much more delightful to touch this, to let his fingers slip through the waves.

She scooted across the seat, putting space between them, but he noticed that she still leaned her head toward his touch. "Mmm."

He did not have to ask what she purred about, and his hormones slipped into overdrive as he tried to figure out what his next romantic move should be. He knew what he wanted it to be, but pulling her into his arms and crushing her on the seat beneath him would only scare her.

It drove him wild when a woman tempted him, then withdrew. Perhaps it worked both ways. Using all his willpower, he put his hands in his lap and resisted the urge to move closer to her.

If it drove her wild, she recovered quickly. On the drive to the summit, she practically glued her nose to the window as the forests of beech, maple, and oak gave way to pine. A misty cloud hung around one peak, and the driver rounded the hairpin turns with care.

"Wow, snow."

He wondered whether a snowball fight could be considered romantic. She had been raised in California, and he was not sure how it was viewed there, or whether they even had snow near where she had lived.

"Do you ski?" she asked.

He laughed. "If I do not, who picked you up when you were ten and insisted you could beat me in a race?"

"Oh, yeah."

"I will never forget. You had snow in your mouth and up your nose. You were all covered in white—"

"Never mind."

He realized he had just taken a step backward in the romance department. "And you looked like an angel."

Her rigid posture softened somewhat.

"You had lost your hat, and your golden hair was all wild around your head, like a halo."

She looked stunned. "I don't remember that."

"Moira, my heart is wounded."

"I...I mean I don't remember losing my hat."

"I picked you up and skied down the mountain with you in my arms, and you said you felt as if you had wings."

"You're making that up!"

He chuckled, pleased that he had been able to win her attention and make her smile. One step back, two steps forward.

"We are almost there."

She looked out the window and oohed and aahed at the view that opened up before them. Miles of pine-covered slopes lay below them now that they had topped the tree line.

"It's beautiful," she said breathlessly.

His heart lurched; he wanted to hear her speak to him in the same breathless tone, and not about some damned view. "Then I am glad I brought you here."

"Yes, thank you. The drive was a wonderful idea."

He did not tell her he had not been referring only to the drive. It was at his request for her hand that her father had brought her back to Ennsway. His promise to marry her and keep her safe.

The limo pulled to a stop at the summit, and Moira reached for the door.

"Button up," William warned. "It is cold and windy."

She pulled her white mink tighter around her throat and donned the matching hat Angela had pushed into her hands before they had left. There had been a tussle over which coat she was to wear today—Moira had not favored the fur—but after a look at Emma, she had given in. William did not understand. Emma had not said a word, just stood there with her hand on her necklace as if she had nothing better to do. But he was glad Moira had worn the fur. She would be warm, and he would have more time to be romantic.

"My God, you can see three hundred sixty degrees up here!" She ran through the snow and hopped onto a flat, sun-cleared rock. "Glacier-carved valleys, moraines. A cirque—is there a lake in it?"

One moment she was twirling around to see everything, the next she was sitting on her rear on the limestone, her hand to her temple.

He rushed to her side and landed on bent knee. "Are you all right?"

"Whew! Just a little light-headed." She laughed—a light, musical sound carried away by the wind. "I forgot about the thin air."

"You must be careful."

"Yes, I will."

"Come, we can sit by the windscreen, and you can look without falling down again."

He led her to the striped windscreen. There was a deeply cushioned seat waiting for them there, with a high back and sides that wrapped around to shelter them further, and just big enough for two people to cuddle on. In front of it was a fire to toast their feet.

William thought Moira looked impressed, but she said nothing as she sat and curled her legs up beneath her coat—on the far side, he noted, not between them.

A footman unfolded a heated blanket on their laps.

"It's warm," she said in surprise.

He handed Moira the temperature control. Her head nearly spun off as she looked around to see what it was plugged into.

"The car, Moira."

"I knew that."

Thermal mugs of coffee were offered, and William scowled at Leonard. If they kept her warm enough, she would not need him to cuddle her.

"Is that a deer?" she asked.

"Where?"

She pointed into the distance, toward a lower slope.

"Yes, I believe so."

Binoculars were offered over Moira's shoulder by yet another silent footman.

"Oh, thank you."

William was beginning to think he had brought along far too many people.

She peered through the binoculars, then took a moment to thank him. "William, you think of everything."

Her smile warmed him far more than the electric blanket, fire, and coffee combined.

She peered through the lenses into the distance again. "It is a deer!" She offered the binoculars to him. "Look."

Her excitement was contagious. Before long, she had him hiking around the summit with her as she pointed out sea fossils.

"You studied this in the United States?"

She nodded. "California's big on geology."

He watched longingly as she traced a fossil with the tip of her finger. If he closed his eyes, he could feel her doing the same on his skin. On his chest. Down his sternum, around his nipple...

"William, you're not enjoying this?"

He worked hard to keep his grin from being lascivious. "Oh, yes. I most certainly am."

"Are you light-headed then?"

"Dreadfully."

She took him by the arm, and he let her lead him back to their cushioned seat. "You should have said something. Here, sit and catch your breath." She tucked the blanket around his thighs, which just led to more delightful images. "I'll be back soon."

He grabbed her wrist. "Where are you going?"

"I've never seen fossils quite like those—"

"Stay." She looked doubtful, so he closed his eyes. "As soon as I catch my breath, I want to study them with you."

"You're interested in geology, too?"

"I own a whole mountain, do I not?"

She laughed at that, and he was able to tug her onto the cushion beside him.

They ate dinner there as the sun set. She melted

against him, allowed him to pull her beneath his arm and share his warmth.

"I wish I had my camera," she whispered.

"We will come back anytime you want," he promised. He turned his head slightly and pressed his lips to her head, only to get a mouthful of mink. "Perhaps when it is warmer."

They remained there a short while, until he promised his hormones it would not be much longer and thus gained control so that he could stand and help her to her feet.

"I hate to go," she said.

"It will be dark in a few minutes."

"I know."

He heard the wistfulness in her reply and knew he had done well today. He had not accomplished his goal, yet, but there was still the drive down the mountain in the dark. The car was chilly inside, which was quite unusual with a driver in attendance and heated seats, but William was not about to complain. Apparently his whole staff had plotted to help him convince Moira to set a date.

He pulled her close and ran his hands briskly over her arms. "Cold?"

She nodded.

"Are your teeth chattering?"

"I th-think so."

"Here, let me warm you." He pulled her tighter, pressed his cheek against hers. *So soft.*

"That's b-better."

"Most definitely."

"What?"

"It warms me, too."

She turned her head—to look at him more closely,

he assumed. Not one to miss an opportunity, he brushed his lips very lightly over hers.

"Your lips are cold," he whispered against them.

"Um..." She ducked her head.

Her breath was warm on his skin and smelled of the sweet cinnamon dessert they had shared. He laid his hand along the side of her face, then let his thumb rest beneath her chin and tilt her head upward until her lips were accessible again.

She did not turn away. Instead, as he dipped his head and covered her lips with his, hers parted softly, allowing him to nibble and taste and caress.

"William..."

Finally, his name on her breathless whisper. His back grew stronger, his shoulders wider, his chest broader. Other parts of his anatomy expanded, too, and he reached around her legs to pull her onto his lap.

The limo lurched to the side, throwing them against her side of the interior with him on top of her. All he could think of after *Boy, my staff is really good* was *one more lurch like that, and he would be cradled in a very nice spot.*

The car continued to do just that. "Rock slide, Your Majesty. I have to swerve to miss the stones."

He nearly strangled trying to compose an appropriate reply to the driver's fabricated story. "Very good. Carry on."

Which was exactly what he intended to do. Oh, he would not steal her virtue in the back of his limo. But he would make her want him to.

"A rockslide?" she queried. "Isn't that danger-ous?"

"Yes, let me protect you." He pressed his body over hers, crushing her into the seat. "Am I too heavy?"

"No."

Ah, that breathy quality again. It made him want to forget they were in the limo with a driver who could hear everything if he wanted to.

A solid thunk against the front fender startled him. "What the hell was that?"

"Rock, sir! Hold on!"

William heard another solid hit, this time on the roof. He vaulted to his knees and looked through the windshield. In the headlights, he could see boulders rolling down the slope and bouncing onto the narrow road. Some continued down the steep drop on the far side. Others came to a halt, threatening to trap the car before they could reach safety. He looked out the back window and saw no lights from the staff cars that had been following.

"There's an overhang ahead, sir!"

"Head for it," William ordered, then realized that was needless. Of course the driver would try to get them to a safe spot.

"Look out!"

In an instant, the headlights were gone.

# Chapter Ten

In total darkness, with the limo headed who-knew-where on the steep mountain road, William's first thought was to save Moira, the future mother of his children. He felt perfectly justified in stretching himself out over her body like a protective blanket. Not that it would do much good if a really large boulder crashed through the roof, but he could keep glass from the windows off her as they broke.

"Keep your eyes closed," he ordered. He jerked at his buttons and spread the front of his coat open wide, making a tent over their heads and upper bodies.

He refused to feel helpless. His driver had grown up in the mountains and was as capable as anyone of getting them to safety—if it was at all possible.

He tried not to relish the feel of her pliant body beneath his; it did not seem like the appropriate time. But her face was warm against his throat. Her breasts pushed against his chest. Her pelvis cradled his. Their legs tangled together. And every lurch of the limousine jolted him against her, making it impossible for him to think of anything else.

"You smell good," he whispered in her ear. "Like a coconut."

"Great." Her breath penetrated his shirt and warmed his collarbone. "We're going to die, and you think I smell good."

There was too much at stake, for both their countries, for them to be wiped off the face of the map like this. He had worked it all out so carefully, and King Albert had been persuaded that it was the right thing to do.

"We will not die. I will not allow it."

"Oh, goody." She twisted beneath him and shoved against his chest.

"Lie still," he crooned.

"Get off of me."

"Not until the danger is past."

She shoved harder. "We've stopped moving, William. Get off."

He raised his head to find that, indeed, the limousine was still. What was left of it, anyway. The driver turned the lights on inside to reveal that the roof pressed in on them a foot lower than it used to be on the passenger side. All the windows were broken from the pressure; glass littered their coats, the seats, the carpet.

"Are you all right, Your Majesty? Sir? Ma'am?" The driver sounded dazed.

William heard no more rocks tumbling down the mountainside, threatening them. As Moira pushed him away, he turned over, braced himself and kicked at the door until it gave way. "We can get out now. Be careful of the glass."

He crawled out, then grasped her trim ankles and slid her gently along the seat until she could sit up and step out—right into his waiting arms. He brushed glass out of her hair, off her shoulders. He had protected her, and he felt very much like a knight in shining armor who had saved his lady and earned her undying gratitude.

The driver kicked open his own door and joined them as the moon peeked out from its cloud covering. "In all my years, I've never seen anything like that, Your Majesty. Definitely not natural."

William plucked more glass out of Moira's hair. "Now do you believe someone is trying to kill you?"

She swatted his hands away.

"I do not want any glass to scratch you." It would be a shame to mar such beautiful skin. He reached for the front of her mink to find and release the hooks.

She slapped at his hands.

"Moira, give me your coat. I will shake it out."

She placed her hand square on his chest and fully extended her arm between them. It was difficult to gauge the look in her eyes in the fleeting moonlight, but he did not think it was warm and grateful.

"It is all right now, Moira," he crooned. "The rock slide is over. We are safe."

"Safe?" It sounded like an accusation. "You think someone's trying to kill me, and I should feel *safe?*"

"Yes, it is all ri—"

"No, it's not all right!" She whirled away from him and stumbled over a small rock, but righted herself against the fender and shook him off again as he tried to pull her into the safety of his embrace. "No one ever tried to kill me before I got contracted to marry you."

"That may not be entirely true."

"Do you have a jealous girlfriend or something?"

"No, it is not that."

"Now—" she pulled herself up until her backbone was so rigid he thought it would crack under the pressure "—I demand you void the contract before I *do* get killed."

"Ah, Moira."

"Immediately, William. I mean it."

"I cannot."

"You will!"

"Even if I wanted to, I could not. It is too late."

"Not if I'm not married, it's not."

"You do not understand."

"You got that right."

He was grateful for the small bit of moonlight as she folded her arms across her chest and tossed her hair. Such passion!

"The people of Baesland and Ennsway would not let me void the contract even if I wanted to. Which I do not." He took a chance and stepped closer to her. "Moira, I love you." Then another step.

"No!"

Her arm shot out again, landing smack in the middle of his chest, though he thought it was less rigid this time. He was relieved that his declaration had registered with her.

"You do not believe me?"

"It's just...the adrenaline talking," she said. "Like when people blurt it out during sex and don't really mean it." When he cast a doubtful look upon her, she added, "I learned about these things, you know. Biology 101."

He knew she was rambling, afraid to face his love. Doubtful of it. How could he not understand? Her mother had died when Moira was ten. Her father had sent her away to live in a foreign country, under the care of servants, when she was only twelve. Love was not something she would accept easily.

"Oh, I mean it, Moira." She clapped her hands over her ears. Gently but firmly, he dragged them away. "And we will not have sex."

"Oh?"

He shook his head. "No, we will make love."

Her lips formed an "Oh," but no sound escaped them.

"All night long," he promised.

"You just—" Her voice squeaked, and she cleared her throat and started over. "You just want my country."

"That is not all I want." He looked around them, gauging the darkness. "But, in the morning, let me show you why your country is important."

CHLOE RELIVED the evening over and over. Before she fell asleep that night. In her dreams. And in between her dreams, when she couldn't sleep.

Her total, overwhelming reaction to him when he'd spread himself on top of her. She knew he'd been playing at the beginning, that he hadn't believed his driver when he first told him he'd swerved to miss a rock. Though what he'd thought his driver was up to was beyond her.

Her sense of protectedness when he'd spread his coat over her. That had been quick thinking on his part. And it had all been for her, when he could just as easily have thrown himself on the floor, pulled the coat over his own head and left her to fend for herself.

Her fear when he'd said he loved her. Fear that he meant it, or that he didn't? She wasn't sure. She tossed and turned on it all night, and still didn't have the answer. As long as he wanted her country, she would never know whether she was just part of the package.

He'd said she would understand better when he explained it all. By dawn, she was ready to hear whatever he had to say, see whatever he had to show her. She knew her country was in ruin compared to his, so what could he want with it? Mining rights? What had Hilda said? Ennsway men would get jobs, children would go to school, and Baesland would get farmland.

If William didn't love her for herself, Baesland could lease their damned farmland!

She got up, got dressed, threw open her door and stormed out. One step, then she tripped over a man-at-arms sleeping on the floor.

He jumped to his feet, blinked his eyes and stood quite rigid. "Your Majesty!"

The toe of her sneaker tapped the floor in short little jabs. "Did you forget where your bed is?"

"Uh, no, Your Majesty. His Majesty ordered me to stay the night here."

"You're from Baesland, aren't you?" Even if his uniform hadn't identified him, she could have told by his speech that he had more education than any man-at-arms she'd met in her own castle.

"Yes, Your Majesty."

"And what were your orders?"

"To keep you safe, Your Majesty."

Like she believed that. "Uh-huh." More like he was put there to keep tabs on her. "Go find His Majesty and tell him I'm ready."

"Yes, Your Majesty."

Since he ran off to do her bidding, she had to concede that he might have been stationed there by William for her protection. Good thing she hadn't needed it.

An hour later, she met William at his limousine. After his make-love-all-night-long promise, she was tempted to tell him they'd take separate cars, but that was silly. She scooted in next to him. Not too close; not too far. If she'd been pressed up against her own door, and he his, she'd still have felt the currents sparking between them.

"Did you sleep well?" he asked.

"Was the guard to protect me or keep me in?"

He scooted halfway across the seat toward her, extended his arm along the back until she felt his fingers playing with the ends of her hair. "If I wanted to keep you in, I would do it myself."

She jerked her head to free her hair, but she could feel his touch all the way up to her roots. His thigh inched closer, and she shot out her hand to stop him. But, with her hand on his thigh, she could no more form a logical refusal than she could sleep last night.

For two hours, he showed her the rich farmlands and idle people Ennsway had to offer. Then he showed her the natural resources and social programs Baesland offered in return, if the border between their countries was dissolved.

It was quite clear that he would marry whoever happened to be in a position to bring him what he wanted—more land. And that happened to be she.

"I see," she said when he concluded their tour. When she glanced at him, saw the warmth in his eyes, she had a moment of doubt about what she had just deduced. Was she wrong?

"It was your father's wish that we be married within three months of the contract date."

"Yes, I read it."

His laugh was low and self-amused. "Yes, I thought

you might have. I know how you like to read and study things."

"I don't want to get married, William."

"But tradition dictates you follow your father's wish."

A sharp laugh escaped her. "Well, you know what I think about tradition, don't you?"

"Ah, yes. Royal brouhaha."

"Exactly."

"Think about this, Moira. Your people want and need revenue. My people want and need expansion. They are all committed to the marriage contract one hundred per cent. If you refuse to marry me, tradition dictates there will be sanctions on both sides. And war."

She couldn't believe it. "War? Surely you exaggerate."

"And if that does not get your attention, there is always my dungeon."

Her lips moved, but she found herself speechless—a rare thing for her.

"You may choose whichever cell you think is less…damp, I believe you said?"

"You can't be serious!" She searched for a solution, reaching for her old standby of what a princess of old might have done in just this situation. Well, actually, that was all too clear. She would have let them war it out over her. Not a bright prospect.

"Or I suppose I could lock you in the tower instead."

"Okay, fine."

"This means yes?"

"It means I'll marry you, but I won't sleep with you."

## *Chapter Eleven*

Chloe pretended that she'd gotten used to William being around in her castle all the time, but that was hardly the case. She was civil when they ate together, which was every meal. If she didn't show up in the atrium for breakfast, her favorite place, he came to her sitting room. If she missed a different meal, he tracked her down.

The truth was, she enjoyed it as much as any game she'd ever played. Hide-and-seek, only she didn't mind getting caught. She was resigned to the fact that she *had* to marry him, and his plans to improve the countries sounded like no less than she would want to do herself, but, honestly, couldn't the man swallow his pride and *ask*?

She saddled her mare and went riding alone, for all of ten minutes. She knew that if she'd asked anyone else to tack up for her, William would have been there before she departed. As it was, he loped up behind her before she'd gotten two miles.

"Moira, I am hurt you did not invite me."

She believed that about as much as she believed he was going to marry her and *not* entice her to share his bed. "Yeah, right. I wanted to be alone."

"I will keep silent."

She noticed half a dozen men riding up behind them, at a discreet distance. William kept his mount beside hers and, true to his word, said nothing. Not that she noticed, she was so lost in memories of how it had felt to ride double with him. She didn't even know she'd turned for home until her mare perked up. Which was a good thing, because, on foot, Chloe never could have found her way back.

Only when the stable was in sight did William speak again. "Have you seen the ballroom?"

"You've done something with my ballroom?"

"Not I, Moira. Meet me there in an hour."

She didn't wait an hour, as he'd undoubtedly known she wouldn't, because he was already there after she rushed through her shower. His hair was damp, his clothes were fresh, his grin was as lopsided as ever as he threw the doors open.

Inside, the ballroom was full of tables. And on every table was an arrangement of the most exquisite possessions anyone could want. Perfume in crystal bottles with gold caps. A sapphire-and-diamond necklace, with matching earrings and bracelet. Rich silks that shimmered beneath the chandeliers. To one side stood a life-size marble sculpture that she was certain must have come from a Greek museum.

She wandered through the room, drinking it all in. Inlaid jewelry boxes, monogrammed gold flatware. Pearls, rubies. A Fabergé egg, just sitting there on the table as if it didn't belong under glass on a high shelf—in a locked room.

*A tiara!* She paused by it and surveyed the entire room. "My God, where did all this come from?"

"All over the world."

She looked closer and saw, beside each gift, a small card that extended best wishes and announced the giver.

"We must memorize these," William told her.

Her eyebrows lifted. "And this is because...?"

"So we are able to thank our guests personally at the wedding ball. It would be rude not to be well-informed and grateful."

"It's not that I'm not grateful. I just can't possibly remember all this." She didn't want to admit she didn't even know what many of the items were. She'd never seen such wealth.

He followed her from table to table, a teasing little bounce in his step. "What? The student in you has not learned tricks to memorize details?"

She spread her arms to take everything in. "Have you looked at how much is here?" She picked up a name card. "And I couldn't pronounce this in a million years."

"Mmm, the shah. Yes, he will be here, I am certain."

"Old buddy of yours?"

William shrugged. "And this is only part of what we have received. There are many more at Baesland Castle."

"Good Lord. I could sell all this and build a hundred schools."

"Do not even think it."

She was drawn back to the tiara.

"Do you like it?"

She ran the tip of her finger over the sparkling diamonds. "It's beautiful. It's the only thing I've seen here without a name beside it."

"It was my mother's. She was married in it, and it was her wish that someday my bride would wear it."

She pursed her lips in thought. His mother probably would turn over in her grave to have an impostor wear her wedding tiara.

"My mother was quite fond of you, you know. Please consider it."

She didn't have to. It would serve no purpose to refuse. "I'll be happy to." When she saw his chest puff out proudly, she was glad she'd agreed.

William left her side, then, and circled the table. "Once we have these memorized, the wedding gifts will probably begin arriving."

Her mouth dropped open, she was sure. "Wedding gifts? Wh-what are these?"

"Engagement gifts, of course."

CHLOE STOOD on a low pedestal in the middle of the sewing room. She watched the minute hand on the clock creep around the dial twice, while three women measured and pinned and stitched. It seemed like two days, not two hours. Her back ached. Her head reeled. Her stomach rumbled.

"Oh, no no no!" Brigitte, the head seamstress, said. When she'd arrived from Paris, Chloe had thought her accent delightful. Now she was sick of it. "You must not eat. If you do, you will soon be bigger than I can let out."

Along with a less active life-style, Chloe blamed the rich food she'd been served at every meal for the five pounds she'd gained. She admitted she had a sweet tooth, and it had never been so well indulged in all her life.

"I need a break, ladies."

"Just a little longer."

Emma patted her hair, and Chloe insisted. "Unbutton me now."

They treated her dress as if it were made of blown glass, all three of them lifting it off her instead of letting her step out of it.

It *was* beautiful, and it wasn't even finished yet. The ladies had sewn on a zillion pearls already, but insisted there were as many more to go. The veil had been attached to William's mother's tiara and sat on a higher pedestal in a corner of the room, as if it were on a throne.

Chloe slipped into her jeans and sweater, ignored the fact that the jeans had grown uncomfortably tight in the waist, and headed for the garden for some peace and quiet. Emma followed silently.

Chloe stretched out on her back on the low wall circling the fountain. The cool stone pressed her vertebrae back into alignment. The gurgling water drowned out the French voices that still echoed in her head. The breeze teased her hair and carried delicate floral scents to her nose.

It was with some surprise that she felt something cold and damp against her cheek. It reminded her of Friday's nose, and Chloe wasn't too surprised when she turned her head and stared into the large brown eyes of a German shepherd. Its leash led up to Louis.

"How are you today?" he asked.

Out of the corner of her eye, she noticed Emma making strange hand gestures that had nothing to do with their pre-arranged signals. Chloe decided it might be wise to get her face out of the dog's reach before she got slobbered to death, so she sat up. "Fine, Louis. I didn't know you had a dog."

He grinned and sat beside her. "He is for you." He patted her knee. "I worry about you, Moira. I agree with Father. I think you're in danger."

"So you're giving me a dog?"

Emma nearly twisted her necklace off. It didn't matter, though. Chloe wasn't ready for another dog; she was still considering flying Friday to Ennsway.

"He'll make you feel safe."

"He catches chandeliers and stops rockslides?"

Louis petted the dog's head and ignored Chloe's sarcasm. "He doesn't frighten you, does he?"

He glanced at her, then, and Chloe noticed that he didn't really see her. It was as if his eyes looked right through her.

"No," she replied. *He* doesn't scare me.

"When you were twelve, I remember you would shudder at the mere picture of a dog."

Emma cleared her throat. "They have wonderful therapists in the United States. Your Majesty, you mentioned that you wanted to freshen up before lunch."

*That* signal Chloe could understand. "Yes, thank you, Emma. Louis, your concern is very touching, but I can't have that dog following me around. I suggest you take him back wherever you got him. Now, if you'll excuse me…"

Louis took the hint and left. The dog lagged behind and took one last look at Chloe over his shoulder, with eyes that threatened to melt her heart and change her mind.

"Be strong," Emma said.

Chloe chuckled. "You know me too well."

Emma's face was transformed by one of her rare smiles. "Yes, Your Majesty."

"So—" Chloe pinned her with an unwavering gaze

"—I figured Anna thought I might take her puppy away because of something her mother had said. And I thought Hilda might have been under the mistaken impression that I didn't like dogs for some reason that escapes me now. But when my brother sneaks up on me with the biggest German shepherd I've ever seen and asks if I'm afraid of it, and you're standing across the room flailing your arms around like a helicopter, it makes me suspicious."

Emma looked at her toes and turned slightly away, as if she'd have liked to flee but knew her place. "Suspicious, Your Majesty?"

"Now would be a good time for you to tell me why I'm supposed to be afraid of dogs."

"Very well." Emma took a deep breath and looked Chloe in the eyes. "But first I must tell you that it is only recently that I put two and two together. You must believe that I would not have put you in this position otherwise."

"Try me."

"Her...your fear of dogs stems from an attack by one of the guard dogs when you were twelve. She... You never knew—*I* never knew, Your Majesty, I swear—that King Albert suspected the attack was an attempt on your life. That's why he sent you away. To keep you safe. I think he originally planned to bring you home again, because he banned all dogs from the country."

"Then why didn't he?"

"Good question. Maybe he never found who was responsible. I swear, I had no idea your life would be in danger. I'm so sorry."

Chloe glanced at the door through which Louis had exited. "Surely my father didn't think it was Louis."

"I'm sure he wouldn't have sent for you if he had. What worries me, Your Majesty, isn't that your brother was responsible, but that he is suspicious that you are so completely over your fear of dogs."

Chloe whispered, "You think he suspects?"

"Perhaps, when…*she* came for the funeral, he saw her. Perhaps there was something familiar about her, something a brother would see that we didn't think of."

"Great. William thinks someone's trying to kill me, and you think Louis is on to our ruse. I'm not so hungry after all."

WILLIAM, taking Leonard's advice again about being romantic, had planned every last detail, except for the clouds obscuring the brilliant nighttime stars he had hoped for. He circled the small table for two on the balcony as he waited for Moira's arrival. The tall white candles flickered, casting a soft light that was, in itself, very pleasing. The bouquet of fresh white roses had been chosen for their mild scent, so as not to compete with the meal.

His staff buzzed around, getting every last detail absolutely perfect.

"Leonard, is it my imagination, or have the staff been whispering among themselves a great deal?"

"Gossip, Your Majesty. Think nothing of it."

"About the wedding?"

"About the bride."

"What about her?"

"It's nothing, Your Majesty." Leonard held out beneath William's glare for all of thirty seconds. "Oh, all right. There's a rumor circulating that she isn't the same person who left here sixteen years ago."

"Of course not. She has grown into a remarkable woman."

"They mean it literally, Your Majesty."

"That is absurd." It was a simple matter for William to dismiss such a ridiculous thought. He had better things to think about. The evening ahead, for instance. And the night.

The small balcony on the third floor of Baesland Castle had been chosen for its intimacy. A nearby heater stood ready to ward off the evening chill. The dining chairs were positioned close to each other, so that when he reached for her hand, it would seem casual and natural. Maybe she would even reach for his.

Just inside the door, where the music could float softly outdoors, sat a harpist. Elsewhere in the castle was a small troupe of town criers, ready to run through the village with their announcement when Moira accepted the engagement ring still burning a hole in his pocket.

If all went well, they would end up together in his suite tonight.

Harp music began with a flourish, then settled into a soft, angelic tune. William thought that was ironic, since his thoughts were anything *but* angelic at the moment. He wanted Moira to wear his ring. He desired her in his bed even more.

Sure, he had originally wanted her, regardless of her looks or disposition, because of the property she would bring him. But now that he had observed her kind manner with small children, he knew no one else could be the mother of his heirs. Now that he had received the sharp edge of her tongue in the dungeon, he knew she cared for people as much as he did—and that she would bring more passion to their marriage than he had dreamed.

And now that her arrival had been announced, he wanted to tell her all that as he proposed, so that she could have the illusion of choosing, as she wanted.

Moira stepped out onto the balcony. One glance at the small table set with candles and flowers, his staff vanishing through the doorway, and her smile told him she knew he was up to something. It did not matter if she knew. What mattered was that she was there, that she was beautiful inside and out—especially out, tonight, in a little black dress that reminded him of his devilish fantasies—and he was prepared to get down on one knee in a proper manner.

"Aren't you afraid we'll get rained on?"

"It would not dare."

A low rumble of thunder answered him. He started to pull out her chair so that they could proceed with the meal before they got drenched, then realized he must be nervous, because he had forgotten his manners. She had not, though. She stepped up to him and waited.

He had kissed the cheeks of hundreds of people. Perhaps thousands. Never had he anticipated one person as much as he did her. Never had his palms sweated before.

"Is something wrong?" she asked.

He brushed his hands against his jacket as casually as possible and hoped the motion went unnoticed. "You will not hold it against me if I enjoy looking at you, will you?"

"Depends on what you're thinking while you're doing it."

"I am thinking how lovely you are. And how happy I am that you accepted my invitation."

"Really, William, you would have hunted me down—"

She fell silent and her teasing smile disappeared as he dipped his head and lightly touched his lips to her cheek. Was he imagining that she turned toward him, that she leaned into his kiss, pressing her cheek more firmly against his mouth? He thought not. Of their own volition, his fingers found their way beneath her chin, tipping it upward so that, on the way to her other cheek, his lips brushed over hers.

He never made it to the other cheek.

Her lips were as soft as he remembered, and, as they parted for him, he hoped there were no ancient vases around for her to knock to the floor and interrupt them again. Her hands, which had flown to his chest the moment he detoured, slipped safely up around his shoulders. When her fingers crept into his hair at the back of his head, he realized he was embracing her so tightly that neither of them could breathe.

He pulled back a hairsbreadth. "Moira, my love—"

Her hands slid down his jacket sleeves as she eased away. "Goodness, is that how you greet all queens?"

He clutched her hands in his, keeping contact. Only the confusion in her eyes told him that she was more affected by his kiss than she would let on.

"You can let go now. I won't break anything, I promise."

Perhaps he had only imagined her confusion, out of hope that her desire matched his. "Are you as hungry as I am?"

"Famished."

He dragged her against him again.

"What are we having for dinner?"

"Dinner?"

She glanced at the table. "Yes, I'm sure you invited me to eat."

He dropped his arms at his sides.

"Or were you hoping I'd be the main course?"

He hung his head and hoped he had not smiled at that suggestion.

"William, I told you I'd marry you, but I won't sleep with you."

He raised his eyes to hers to see whether he could determine just how serious she was about that. If the heat he saw there was any indication, she would soon melt.

Reassured, he grinned as he reached for the back of one of the chairs. "Then we shall dine before it rains."

He was out of luck on that count. They were in the midst of their third course when raindrops plopped into their wine. "We will move inside."

"Actually, I'm finished."

"You eat like a—"

"I know. A finch. You've told me, but it's not true. I'm not used to marathon meals, which, by the way, aren't good for you."

"But I am fit."

She eyed his shoulders and chest appreciatively, and he was glad to draw her attention back to him, though he was still trying to decipher the connection between a meal for hot, sweaty runners and an intimate dinner for two. The hot-and-sweaty part renewed his fantasies.

"Well, if you are finished, perhaps you would like a tour of my castle?" *Say, my suite?*

"I stayed here, remember?"

"Ah, but you did not see everything."

"Such as?"

*An indirect route would be best.* "The gallery holds many fine works of art."

Her brow arched. "You're asking me to see your etchings?"

He wanted to start at the crease on her forehead and kiss her all the way down to her toes, but, knowing how much she appreciated fine art, he answered her straightforwardly. "I do not think there are any etchings there."

She laughed with delight. "It must be an American expression."

He did not care what had made her laugh; he was the one privileged to lean back in his chair and relish the sparks in her eyes that came from more than candlelight, her teasing smile, the tiny pulse point in her throat.

"Okay. I'd love to see your gallery."

She scooted her chair back, and William jumped up to help her with it. Not that she needed it. She was quite the independent American woman, with a mind and muscles of her own. It was all the more to lo...like about her.

The sky opened up, and they dashed for the door before they got drenched.

"The harp music is beautiful," she said.

He regretted that the harpist could not follow them around the castle. It was just as well, though, as he was not going to let anyone else into his suite with them. Whenever he finally got Moira there.

He showed her the gallery, which also housed more gifts. The smallest was a solid-gold quill pen; the largest, a grand piano; the most delicate, a handmade lace tablecloth; the oldest, an eighteenth-century grandfather clock.

Then came the tropical room, which was very tropical and very little actual "room." She was properly astounded by the indoor pool, as some ancestor of his had been very freehanded with the gold leaf on the wall tiles around the deck. He did not show her every room, as he wanted to reach his suite sometime that year.

"So many rooms!"

He indicated that they should turn right. "And my suite is in this wing."

"Oh, uh…I don't believe you showed me the towers."

"The towers," he repeated slowly. "All of them?"

She pursed her lips, then replied, "We can skip the ones along the curtain wall, if you like."

He shrugged as if it were of no importance, which it would not be if he did not ache to get her alone in his chambers. And if he did not have a prisoner—the same man she had ordered released—in a tower she wanted to view.

*Did she suspect?*

"There is really nothing of interest in the towers."

"Oh, but I'd like to see them."

"The electricity is unreliable in bad weather."

"Then bring a flashlight."

"I am sure I do not have one."

"Let's risk it."

"No, I think not. You could trip on the steps in the dark and hurt yourself."

"William…"

"You can see them when the weather clears."

"You don't want me up there, do you?"

"I do not want you to get hurt."

"Well…" She tapped her toe on the marble floor,

and he knew he was in trouble. "If I can't see everything, I might as well go home."

*Do American men have to go through this?* "If you promise to see everything, I suppose I could have someone follow us with a light, just in case."

"What are you up to?"

He strove to look as innocent as a little boy caught near the cookie jar. "Nothing."

"Okay."

"Everything?"

"Well, you don't have to show me any of those closets that used to pass as toilets."

"I promise to leave them off the tour."

He summoned Leonard, who looked very surprised and mumbled what sounded like "Do I have to explain everything?"

"You have taken to muttering in your old age, Leonard."

"Sorry, Your Majesty. I said, do you need anything?"

While Moira admired a hand-carved frieze, William told Leonard about needing a flashlight and, more important, instructed him as to the prisoner.

"What progress has been made on the investigation?"

"Looks like we have the wrong man, Your Majesty. The reports on him, to this point, have all been exemplary."

"Release him, then."

"Very well, Your Majesty."

In a matter of minutes, a flashlight made its way into William's hand, and he led Moira away.

"See?" he asked when she had made a thorough inspection of all four towers.

"I don't know. It feels like someone's been living in this one."

"You think it...feels different?" he asked dubiously.

"It's warmer here than in the others. And it smells like coffee."

He stepped close enough to whisper in her ear. "All I can smell is coconut."

She touched her hair self-consciously as she bolted away from him. "It's my shampoo."

"Yes, I know. Come, there is only my apartment left for you to see."

Her eyes darted around the tower, as if seeking something to hold her there.

"You promised, Moira."

She took a deep breath and stiffened her spine, which just jutted her breasts forward and served to distract him more.

"Okay," she said.

"You act as though there is a firing squad there instead of a Renoir."

"You have a Renoir and didn't tell me?"

He shrugged innocently. "A man likes to save some surprises."

As they exited the door at the bottom of the tower, he pushed the flashlight back into Leonard's hands and told him to get lost. When they reached his suite, he pushed the door open and let Moira enter first, so that she could get an unobstructed view of his favorite painting.

"It's beautiful."

After thirty seconds of that, he no longer wanted her looking at his painting with the same rapt interest she had shown fossils at the summit. He wanted her to be interested in him. As a man. As a lover.

He felt his pocket to be sure he still had the ring. *Check.* He laid his arm around her shoulders in a friendly gesture, and she did not step away. *Check!* He turned her into his embrace and nuzzled the corner of her lips as he reached into his pocket and pulled out the small velvet box.

*Damn, she needs to be seated for this to work right.*

He inched her backward until they reached a chair, any chair, until her knees were against it and she could not move farther. He knew he was supposed to sit her down in it so that he could get on bended knee in front of her, but he could not bear to put space between them.

"Moira," he whispered against her lips, just as his name was on her lips, also.

"William."

When she would have laughed about it, and possibly broken the spell, he traced her bottom lip with the tip of his tongue. Any words she would have spoken were smothered by her soft moan.

"Moira, please, you must sit down."

She clung to him. "Don't want to."

*Checkmate.* "You must."

"Why?"

"I have something to ask of you." He heard knocking, and absently thought it was supposed to be bells ringing. He wanted to tell her he loved her, but he dared not. Not yet. He could not bear to have her tell him that he was just caught up in "the moment" again. He would pick that time very wisely.

"Your Majesty!" His man-at-arms's interruption startled him and made Moira jump.

"Unless you want to be shot at sunrise—"

"Your Majesty, the prisoner has escaped."

"You imbecile!"

"What prisoner?" Moira asked.

The man-at-arms apparently thought his news was more important than his life. "I just went on my shift, sir, and the tower is empty."

*Stalemate!*

# Chapter Twelve

Under normal circumstances, William dressed himself just fine. But today his thoughts raced ahead to the wedding ceremony that was to take place in two hours, and it was thanks only to his valet's handing him his clothing in proper sequence that William managed to don his country's midnight-blue military uniform.

The gold braid hung straight; the brass buttons were polished to a glow. It was said that women could not resist a man in uniform. If that was true, he could only hope this one would do the trick with Moira, the woman he had chosen to be his bride before he really knew her. He had deliberated over asking King Albert for her hand for months. If he had been acquainted with the lovely woman she had grown into, there would have been no deliberation at all. She was the one he wanted, desired, dreamed about.

And he had not slept with her, so no one could accuse him of lust, could they?

He had never planned on *not* sleeping with his queen before the ceremony—much less after, as she had said they would not. He smiled to himself. *That* was a situation he was determined to correct at the earliest possible moment. Preferably tonight.

Leonard appeared at the door. "Your Majesty, His Royal Highness, Prince Louis, would like a moment of your time."

"Show him in."

He guessed Louis had come to shake his hand and wish him well. It was the right thing to do. He had never much liked Louis; he was as selfish as his father had been spineless. If his mother had lived longer, he might have turned out different, although Moira had grown up without their mother and turned out wonderful.

Nearly perfect, except for that damned American independent streak.

"Your Majesty," Louis said as he entered the room. As the man who would give the bride away, he was already dressed in Ennsway's military uniform, the color of trees in deep shade.

"Louis, how nice of you to come see me."

"I feel I must tell you something of utmost importance."

William strove for levity. "Relax. My father explained it all to me years ago." His valet handed him his sword, which he hung at his side.

"Seriously, William, I have shocking news."

"All right. I am listening."

"First you must promise me not to do anything drastic. Not to go off half-cocked until you have all the facts."

*Had King Albert's prediction come true?*

Fear gripped William, and he strode across the room, tempted to grab Louis by the throat. "If anything has happened to Moira, I swear—"

"That's just it. I don't know where *Moira* is."

"She is missing?"

"No. Yes. You don't understand." Louis paced the carpet.

"Spit it out, man!"

Louis glanced around at the curious valet and Leonard. "Dismiss your staff, please."

At a jerk of William's head, the men disappeared.

Louis continued in a tone laced with both apology and outrage. "The woman in Ennsway Castle, the woman getting ready to marry you today, is not my sister."

William took a step back, as if that would give him a clearer picture of this confusing accusation. It was one thing for the staff to gossip about it; it was quite another for her own brother to deny her.

"She is not Moira, I tell you."

It took William a moment to let it sink in, to disbelieve it, to find his voice. "And on what do you base this...suspicion?"

"It's more than that. I've felt uncomfortable with her since the day she arrived. I knew something was not right, I just couldn't put my finger on it. And then I saw her with the dog, and she didn't cry or shake. She petted it." He sounded as if that were unbelievable.

William felt a moment of relief as he began to doubt the man's sanity. "So she is not afraid of dogs anymore."

In a tight voice, Louis said, "So you noticed it, too."

"I noticed nothing of the kind."

"You don't know my sister as well as I do. She's not the same."

William thought one of them should remain calm. One of them should be reasonable. "She has been gone sixteen years, Louis. Over half her life."

"I would still know she isn't my sister. She isn't

Ennsway's queen. She isn't the woman promised to you by my father.''

William took up pacing when Louis stopped, his logic racing as fast as he covered the carpet. "She does not want to marry me. If she were not Moira, she would not go through with this wedding."

"So she says. But think about it. A stranger gets the opportunity to be a queen."

*Ah, a hole in Louis's argument.* "She is already queen."

"Then she gets to marry you."

"I told you, she does not want to marry me."

Louis snickered. "Get real, William. Any woman wants to be richer than she already is."

"I do not believe you."

"Then think on this. She's an impostor, I'm sure of it. The foolish woman knows nothing about running a country—that was obvious when she eliminated the death tax. This way, she'll have *you* to run the country for her."

"Enough!"

"Think on it." Louis's vehemence was palpable.

*Life without Moira?* William's hands itched to throttle the prince. "You should leave now."

"I'll be at the castle. You call me, and I'll put a stop to this wedding, but I can't do it without your support. There would be a revolt, I'm afraid." Louis exited the room as neatly as an actor leaving the stage.

*Could it be true?* William wondered whether it was worth putting off his wedding night over a silly rumor.

Or was she an impostor? Was he marrying the wrong woman? And once he had, when she was discovered, what would happen to Baesland-Ennsway, the new country being formed?

*Preposterous!*

Such a thing could not happen. Emma would have known. And just why had Emma disappeared for days? Had she really been dismissed? And by whom?

Good God, had he fallen in love with the wrong woman?

CHLOE LINGERED over her brunch, putting off the moment when she would have to shed her robe, climb up on the pedestal that had been moved to her sitting room, and let Angela and the French women hook her into her wedding gown.

She should have been looking forward to this, her wedding day. Instead, she'd spent the early morning with her new minister of education, redefining the educational standards for Ennsway's children. With or without William's help, illiteracy in Ennsway was going the way of the dinosaurs. By midmorning, she'd selected half a dozen rooms in the castle and outlined her plans to devote them to child care.

She should have had the same freedom to choose the man she wanted for her husband. Not that she wouldn't have chosen William, but, for heaven's sake, what did she have to do? She'd given him hours of her time the other evening. An intimate dinner, a tour-for-two of his castle, a romantic clinch in the privacy of his apartment. And had the man once gotten down on his knee?

No-o-o-o-o, he hadn't.

Had he produced an engagement ring?

No-o-o-o-o, he hadn't.

Had he once even begun a sentence with "Moira, it would do me great honor if…"?

No-o-o-o-o, he hadn't done that, either. What was he waiting for? For her to ask him?

Well, that had merit. Had the circumstances been different, had she not been signed away like a dairy cow or a bushel of corn, she might have considered it. But it really was his place to do the asking in this case.

She knew she should tell him she wasn't who he thought she was. But then he wouldn't be contracted to marry her. Then he wouldn't propose for sure; he'd go find the real Moira so that he could marry her and get the damned land. Then he wouldn't have the woman who loved him, because Chloe loved him more than any other woman ever could.

Moira wouldn't care about William's social programs or the building improvements that would raise the standard of living for thousands of people in both countries. As much as Chloe liked Moira, she knew the princess had been spoiled from infancy on and expected things to be done for her, not *by* her.

So, as she lingered over tea and pastry, she still debated whether and when to tell William the good news–bad news, depending on how one looked at it.

"Please, Your Majesty," Angela said shyly, though she had grown more confident with her English over the past few weeks. "It is growing late."

"I don't want to rush. Those French ladies—" Chloe glanced across the room at them, still poofing and primping silk and lace "—aren't about to let me sit down once I have that gown on."

Her wedding dress had turned out even more beautiful than the sketch. It was the one design William had shown her that she wasn't able to label, without a second thought, as hideous. He must have known. He must have seen it in her eyes or sensed her hesitation before she disparaged it. As if any woman in her right mind wouldn't have fallen immediately in love with the silk, lace, and pearl work of art.

"You're not worried about the rumor, are you?" Angela asked.

Chloe, about to sip her tea, set the cup back in its saucer. "What rumor?"

Angela glanced around, as if debating whether to continue now that she'd begun. She shrugged, as if what she had to say carried little importance. "I've heard whispers that you are not King Albert's real daughter." She rushed to assure her queen, "Of course, I don't believe this."

Chloe slowly became aware that the rattling noise she heard was her hand shaking the cup against the saucer. As if she'd been burned, she snapped her hand away to the safety of her lap.

"Who do these people say I am, Angela?" She noticed Emma playing with her long strand of pearls, warning Chloe not to go there.

"Oh, they don't say, Your Majesty. It is nothing. Just whispers. It would not matter."

"It wouldn't matter if I were someone else?"

Emma went way past fingering her necklace. It ended up wound around her neck tightly, like a noose, and Chloe wondered if they hanged impostors in this country.

"Angela, ladies..." Emma addressed everyone in the room. "Her Majesty would like a few moments alone before she gets dressed." Once they were all gone, Emma turned on Chloe. "Are you out of your mind?"

"What do you want me to do?"

"Think about where you want to spend the night. In

the dungeon or the tower? Because, if you confess, that's where you're going to end up for sure.''

''I don't know, Emma.''

''Well, I do! What is going through your mind?''

Chloe's shoulders lifted in defeat. ''I love him.''

''Then marry him and make him the happiest man alive. Don't push him into a corner where he has no choice but to put you in chains.''

Chloe hoped that was an exaggeration, though she hadn't known Emma to be given to that. Would the man Chloe loved do that to her?

Well, sure, if he didn't love her back.

''Get up on that pedestal,'' Emma ordered. ''I'm going to call the ladies back in. You're going to get dressed and get married—on schedule.''

Chloe sighed, slowly got to her feet and dropped her robe in her chair. Emma hadn't steered her wrong so far. Chloe resigned herself to the fact that, for once, except for the barest of lingerie necessary to preserve her modesty, other people were actually going to dress her.

She wasn't allowed to put on her own stockings— she ''might snag them.'' Angela donned white gloves for the task, though Chloe did fight for and win the right to hook her own garters. She stepped into a slip when told to do so. She sucked in when told to do so. She turned when told to do so.

And all the while, she gave more thought to what was right and what was wrong. By the time the last hooks were in place, when the last loose pearl had been reattached, when her tiara hugged her head and her tulle veil covered her hair, she knew what had to be done.

And she was the one to do it. She could not lie to the man she loved.

"Emma, I have to see William."

An audible gasp filled the room, from the French seamstresses, Angela, Emma, the ladies-in-waiting, and the maid clearing the table.

"No, it is not possible."

"I have to." She didn't whine or say it in any manner in which Emma might think she had the right to disagree. She was firm in her resolve to do this, and do it right.

"I will arrange a phone call, Your Majesty."

"No."

"It will only take me a moment."

"I have to do this in person."

"It is not in the timetable, Your Majesty."

"I insist."

Emma reached up, grabbed her necklace and yanked it off. Pearls bounced and rolled across the rose-colored carpet like little beads of mercury racing for their freedom. A freedom, apparently, that Chloe was not allowed to enjoy.

Her secretary—her friend!—flung what was left of the strand against the wall. "If you're not going to take my advice, I guess I don't need this anymore."

"Emma!"

"If you get a choice, shall I tell His Majesty you prefer the tower or the dungeon?"

"You can't buffalo me like this. Get me to William, and do it now."

"But, Your Majesty," Angela interjected, "the people have come to see you in your gown. They are waiting for you. You would not be able to get through in a car. Please, Your Majesty, the telephone would be much better.''

Chloe knew that if she called William, he'd want to hear her important news immediately, and it wasn't something she was willing to do over the phone. "No. Emma, send for William. Tell him it's important that I see him before the wedding."

"Do it yourself." Emma walked out.

"Angela—" Chloe turned to her maid "—will you do it?"

Angela, in slack-jawed shock that Emma would disobey her queen, responded quickly. "Of course, Your Majesty."

After Angela rushed away to carry out the order, Chloe abandoned her pedestal and moved, in a cloud of silk that mocked her every step of the way, to the window. A crowd of thousands stood in the courtyard below, waiting for a glimpse of their queen on her wedding day.

*Their queen.*

*Well, darn it, that's me!*

Only, depending on how William took the news, there might not be a wedding. Today—or any day, for her. Emma had threatened her with the dungeon or one of the towers. Chloe wasn't even sure which castle she'd be locked in.

As she looked out at the crowd, she wondered whether she'd have to be kept from them for her own safety. They were in favor of this wedding, this merger of two countries. If her honesty jeopardized that, she might be in more danger from an angry mob than she was from William.

She was too nervous to sit, even if the French ladies would have allowed it. Which was highly unlikely, since they followed her as she paced the room, continually primping and tucking and draping the silk into some preconceived arrangement.

She finally blew up at them. "Would you quit?" But they pretended they'd forgotten any English they'd known during her fittings. The next time one of them reached for an unbecoming wrinkle over her hips, Chloe swatted at the lady's hands.

It seemed forever before William arrived. By that time, Chloe was sure she would be beheaded or burned at the stake. Maybe even drawn and quartered. It didn't alter her decision, though.

William charged through the door as if he feared her life were in danger again. "Your Majesty!" He sounded quite relieved to see that she was still in one piece.

Chloe had to no more than glance around the room to send everyone scurrying out.

"Moira, what is it?"

She walked over to the door to shut it, so that she could say what had to be said without adding fuel to the rumors—if she hadn't already.

William's unwavering eyes followed her carefully as she returned to face him. "You are very beautiful, Moira, but is it not against tradition for the groom to see the bride before...?" He grinned, and his eyes twinkled merrily. "Ah, yes, I remember. Tradition. Royal brouhaha. Never mind. I would rather tell you how radiant you are today. Even more ravishing in that dress than I anticipated. And I must tell you, I anticipated— Moira, stand still. Why are you pacing like that?"

With a deep breath, she gathered her courage, turned

to face him one more time and resolutely planted her feet in one spot. "I have something to tell you."

His eyebrows slowly puckered together. Levity was gone; she held no illusion that he dismissed her mood as prewedding jitters.

One of her feet started to move, but she caught herself before she fell into pacing again. It would be counterproductive, and besides, she was beginning to hate the restrictions of her long, heavy gown. Her slip whispered a soft *Impostor...impostor...impostor* every step of the way.

"I'm not who you think I am."

William's hand shot up. He ripped his military hat from his head and threw it against the wall. He raked his fingers through his hair. But he, also, did not pace. He did not leave her, but stared over her shoulder at the wall behind her. The muscles in his jaw clenched.

"You don't look surprised."

"I have heard rumors."

*Look at me.* "You didn't believe them?"

"I do not listen to gossip."

*Look at me!* "William—"

"And then your brother...then Louis came to me this morning and told me his suspicions."

*Please.*

When he finally looked her in the eyes, the intensity of his gaze was so powerful that she was uncertain whether to be thankful or to run and hide.

"Will you let me explain?"

"Have I not been patient with you these past weeks? Have I lost my temper with you? Why would you ask if I would let you explain?"

"Maybe because your hand's on your sword."

His reply, as he threw both hands up in the air, was

an enraged growl that illustrated what Chloe thought to be the highest level of anger a man could reach and still not kill someone. But at least his sword was still sheathed.

She stared at the top button of his uniform and noticed the furious pounding of the pulse in his neck.

"Who are you?"

"Chloe Marshall."

"The American woman? Your friend?"

She nodded.

"You simply...switched places?"

"Yes."

"When you were twelve?"

"No."

"Fourteen?" His voice rose when she shook her head. "Sixteen? Twenty? When?"

"A week before I flew home...here."

"Good God." He turned away.

She stared at the breadth of his back as he walked slowly to the window. He stood tall and proud, neither slump-shouldered nor defeated. He would be tough with her, she knew. She had insulted him and his throne and every person in his country and hers by playing this game with Moira.

"I think your brother is insane."

She must have misunderstood. "What?"

He continued to stare out the window. "I said I think your brother is insane."

*Not "Louis," but "your brother."* She felt the first seed of hope. "And this means...?"

"I did not believe him when he came to me this morning." He looked at her. "I did not want to."

"And now?"

"Oh, I have given the matter a great deal of thought."

*Since this morning?*

"At first I wondered if it could be true. And then I realized I do not care."

She couldn't look away from his eyes, which didn't so much as waver. She felt herself drawn across the room toward him, first one slow step, then another. And yet another—each stride quicker and longer than the one before. It would be a cruel trick for him to look at her like that, then toss her out the window. Was she willing to risk it?

*Yes.*

"After all, what good is merging our kingdoms if I do not have you by my side?"

"You mean—"

He opened his arms and swallowed her whole. He whispered tenderly, "I mean, Moira, that I want you. I want none other." Holding her hand, he dropped down onto his knee in front of her. "Will you do me the honor of marrying me?"

Tears blurred her vision. She couldn't see the wall, the window; she could barely see him. Was he asking because he still wanted to merge the kingdoms? Or had he meant what he said, that Baesland-Ennsway would mean nothing to him with a different woman—the original Moira—by his side?

"Oh, William..."

"You have to think this over?" he asked dryly.

She laughed and sniffed. "No, of course not."

"Damn it, woman, say yes."

"Yes!"

He reached into his pocket. "I have carried this with me for too long—it seems like eternity—waiting for the right moment. I had wanted to court you properly first, before your father told you about our contract.''

He slipped the most beautiful ring she'd ever seen onto her third finger. Like William, it was one of a kind.

And the fact that he'd been carrying her engagement ring around with him, waiting for the perfect moment, spoke of the love he hadn't mentioned.

CHLOE FOUND HER WAY unerringly through the castle to the great hall and out the main door. Not that she could have gone more than a foot in the wrong direction, with all the ladies-in-waiting and footmen accompanying her. Outside, standing in brilliant sunshine, were thousands of people who cheered her presence. Children waved, women cried, men called out good wishes.

An open carriage awaited her. Its four snow-white horses stood with their ears pricked attentively, the near leader's postilion rider in a scarlet coat and white breeches. Black leather harness shined, as did its silver embellishments. White ribbons streamed from each bridle and from intricately braided manes.

Emma waited beside the carriage. Chloe paused in front of her and smiled tentatively. ''I don't have to fire you or something to save face, do I?''

Emma's smile was as warm as her tone, and relieved Chloe immensely. ''No, Your Majesty. I'll tell everyone you flogged me in private.''

Flogging! She'd forgotten that one when she reviewed everything William might have done to punish her.

''Ride with me?''

"It would be my honor, Your Majesty. You are truly a queen to be proud of."

It took all three French ladies to get Chloe into the carriage with no rips or snags, and as few wrinkles as possible. She was glad she didn't understand a word of their language as they babbled on and on. Chloe took the seat facing forward; Emma rearward.

Chloe noticed that her friend wore no necklace, and she wasn't about to suggest she replace it anytime soon.

"I feel naked without it," Emma said.

"I wasn't going to say anything."

"You were staring at my neck. I never used to wear one. Somehow it became a habit."

"I'm sure you'll get used to going without again."

"Yes, I think it's time. Your instincts are good. And I'll still be on hand."

The carriage rolled forward. Chloe smiled and waved at the crowd as she set out for the small church just the other side of the border between Ennsway and Baesland. A border that, in an hour or so, would no longer exist.

"Good, because I have a question."

"Yes, Your Majesty?"

"Is it right for us not to tell the people?"

"According to the grapevine, they would prefer you didn't. They're getting exactly what they want out of this marriage."

Chloe studied their faces as she passed by them. Smiling, cheering, crying. Unemployed, illiterate, anticipating a better future for their children.

"If you told them, there would be months of turmoil while they decided what to do about it. In the end, they would accept you and get on with progress."

"You're certain?"

"It's a small country, and I have a lot of relatives. I'm sure."

It was difficult to carry on a conversation over all the cheering. Chloe fell into an awed silence until she got a good look at their route. A really good look. "There're carpets on the road." Laid end to end, they stretched out as far as she could see. All colors, all patterns, all sizes.

"It's tradition."

"But—"

"One you should not dispense with."

"But the horses—"

"Were exercised before we left. Smile."

Chloe resumed smiling and waving.

"It's the people's way of taking part of your wedding home with them. Many of these rugs were begun the day you were born. Others were crossed thirty years ago by your mother's wedding carriage. So you see, if they didn't want you, they wouldn't have gone to the trouble."

Every fifteen feet, a different child dipped into a basket and tossed confetti into the air. Small, bright bits of paper landed on the horses' backs and beneath their silent hooves. Others fluttered into the carriage and decorated Chloe's lap, like a king's ransom in jewels scattered over a white sheet.

At the border, twelve trumpeters heralded her arrival into Baesland. Mounted men-at-arms, with polished black boots up to their knees and smiles from ear to ear, greeted her carriage and preceded it the rest of the way. Here, in Baesland, rose petals were tossed. Flagpoles displayed white silk banners, bearing Moira's and

William's entwined initials, that fluttered in the breeze. Baskets of flowers cascaded from every lamp post.

"You look like you're enjoying this," Emma pointed out.

"Why wouldn't I?"

"Uh...tradition?"

Chloe shrugged. "I never said all tradition was bad."

"Do the words *royal brouhaha* ring a bell?"

"Sometimes it has its place."

"Uh-huh."

Chloe couldn't imagine giving this up, especially not William. Moira was welcome to broken appliances, the wrong checkout line, and vehicles that broke down. She could have an overdrawn checking account, past-due notices, and auto insurance companies that threatened to cancel. Let her deal with mucking out stalls and bartering time on horseback.

The carriage turned onto a side road for a mile, then came to rest in front of a large, impressive church. Rose petals covered the carpet leading along the walk and up the steps to the door. No sooner had the toe of Chloe's shoe touched the ground than a fanfare of trumpets announced her arrival with such magnitude that she was sure all of Europe had just jumped out of their skins.

Louis crooked his elbow for her and smiled. He even looked as though he hadn't gone to talk to William that very morning about his suspicions.

"Shame on you, Louis," she said.

"What?"

"Telling William I'm not your sister."

"Apparently he didn't believe me."

"I could have you punished, you know."

"For making an honest mistake? Now, Moira, you wouldn't be so cruel." He patted her hand, which was resting lightly on his arm, with his scarred one.

"Don't test my patience."

Cameras flashed repeatedly. Foreign news cameras recorded every detail of her appearance and every blink of her eyes. The pipe organ belted out a full, rich tune. Chloe tried to identify it as Bach or Handel, but she'd been miserably poor in music appreciation.

"That's our cue," Louis said. He escorted her up the steps, through the door, to the beginning of the long white runner.

They paused, giving the French ladies time to straighten her gown and long train. The media was all left behind. A footman handed her a cascade of roses, stephanotis, and lilies of the valley.

Sunlight behind the tall stained-glass windows cast brilliant colors on the people waiting inside and the white runner, giving her the impression of walking into a giant jewel box. And she was the center of attention.

William, standing tall and proud and regal, waited for her at the other end. Anna, sans puppy, began the procession, followed by attendants Chloe had never met. Her maid of honor was supposedly a cousin, when she would rather have had Moira. But, of course, that was out of the question.

All that really mattered waited for her—William. Her groom. Her husband-to-be.

She could think of nothing else as she drew nearer to him, as she took his strong arm, stood beside him with confidence and repeated her vows. She hesitated over the "obey" part, and glanced up to see his eyes dancing over her predicament.

"Do not worry," he whispered to her. "We both know you will not."

If she hadn't already fallen in love with him, that would have done it. She repeated the vows, word for word.

The ceremony passed in a blur, even as Chloe struggled to commit it all to memory. The scent of roses and lilies of the valley should have overpowered William's herbal shampoo, but Chloe knew it so well, she could detect it.

He stood tall and proud beside her, yet she was aware of the thoughtfulness behind his every gaze in her direction. When he took her hand in his, she felt warmth, strength, tenderness. When they turned together to face the people, she knew, as William's queen, what was expected of her.

And she remembered, belatedly, that in a moment of foolishness, she'd also sworn that she would not sleep with him.

# Chapter Thirteen

Guests filled the state dining hall at Baesland Castle. Chloe met more people in the span of an hour than she had in her whole life, and she was expected to smile, say something personal to each one, and forget about ever having a moment to herself again.

She didn't mind strolling through a hall the size of Texas on William's arm, or meeting enough aunts, uncles, and cousins to populate the state. She didn't mind sitting next to him at a table so long she couldn't see the people at the other end, because he bumped knees with her repeatedly. Nor did she mind kissing him whenever the crowd, which grew increasing rowdy on champagne, demanded it.

On the contrary, she enjoyed it all immensely. Someday her daughters would celebrate similarly—if she could figure out how to sleep with her husband without looking as if she were backing down from all her principles.

The ball began two hours later. Thankfully, Emma had sneaked a few ballroom dancing lessons in with Chloe when she'd finally faced the fact that the wedding was a certainty.

When the music began, William led her onto the dance floor.

"I'm a bit rusty," she whispered. It wouldn't have mattered if she'd majored in dance. Once her hand was in his, his other on her waist, she couldn't be expected to keep her mind on him and where her feet were going at the same time.

"Just follow me," he murmured.

*Anywhere.* If only he'd ask.

"Relax, Moira. Let the music take you."

*Easier said than done.* But he was superbly graceful, and he swept her away in a waltz as other couples joined them.

"Did I tell you that you are the most beautiful woman here tonight?" he asked.

She felt her cheeks grow hot, and it had nothing to do with the amount of energy she expended trying not to step on his feet.

"It is true," he added. "I have never seen a bride so radiant."

"You've never seen one so embarrassed."

He leaned closer. "I have never seen one so right for me. I want to tell all these people to go home so we may begin the honeymoon."

She glanced around to see if he had been overheard. While his soft tone couldn't have been picked up, his closeness to her ear hadn't escaped notice. Nearby women smiled knowingly. Wistfully.

"You will not turn me down tonight, will you, Moira?"

She stepped on her own foot and staggered.

William simply pulled her closer to him and steadied her, as if he did it every day. "How clumsy of me," he said, loud enough for those around them to hear.

"Forgive me, my darling. If I do it again, you may trade me in next dance." Then, softer: "You did not answer me. Will you turn me down tonight?"

She'd put him off so long, she felt like a virgin.

He cocked his head and studied her. "Why do you look at me that way?"

"I've never met a truer gentleman than you."

"That is not how it looks to me."

"Oh? How does it look?"

He licked his lips. "Like I am an ice cream cone and you want to taste me with your tongue."

She grinned. "Careful. If you make me trip again, I'm honorbound to trade you in. I have witnesses."

"If you continue gazing at me that way, your witnesses will begin leaving without my asking."

Her grin broadened, and she hoped she didn't look like a sappy fool. "Couldn't be soon enough for me."

"Oh? What do you want to do?"

"Well, if you were an ice cream cone, you'd be melting in my hot little hands, and I'd have to lick you all over."

He stumbled.

AT TWO O'CLOCK in the morning, Chloe still hadn't grown tired of playing cat-and-mouse games with William on the dance floor. Their banter was no more than a prelude to what was to come after. She knew that. From the heated look in his eyes, he knew it, too. And at 2:00 a.m., he was done playing.

"It is growing late," he said.

"I could dance all night."

"We already have."

Knowing she was safely in the midst of hundreds of people, she'd grown bold. "You're tired?"

He laughed. "I have never been less tired, my love. Come. We shall bid our guests good-night."

When they actually began to thread their way, arm in arm, across the ballroom and toward the door, Chloe kept up a brave front, though her courage was failing. What if he'd been teasing her? Acting as a bridegroom should act in public, but remembering what she'd said about not sleeping with him? What if he abandoned her at the door of her own apartment?

Truthfully, she didn't remember ever feeling quite like this—not even before her first sexual experience. And, pretty sure that Moira had saved herself all these years out of some sense of royal obligation, Chloe wondered just what William thought he was getting.

One thing they didn't have to discuss—it was a safe bet they weren't going to be practicing birth control. What king didn't want heirs?

He paused, and she stopped reflecting on the night ahead long enough to realize they had reached the door to his apartment. The night ahead was here. He pushed open the door, gathered her up in his arms, carried her in and kicked the door shut behind them.

"Ah, we are alone."

She tried to think of witty banter, but didn't have time before his lips closed over hers in an all-too-brief but powerful kiss.

"I am so hungry for you, Moira." He set her on her feet and turned her away from him. "How do I get you out of this dress?"

"It has buttons and hooks."

"Good God, there must be a million of them." His fingers traced the buttons over her spine, from nape to waist. "And they are so tiny."

She stepped away from him and offered, "I'll call Angela."

He dragged her back against his chest. His wine-scented breath teased her hair. His voice rumbled in her ear. "You would not deny me the pleasure of undressing my wife, would you?"

Relieved that he hadn't been playing with her all evening just to dump her at her doorstep, she reached behind her and lifted her hair off her neck. "Start here."

Instead, his hands slid over the front of her gown, along her ribs, up, until his palms covered her breasts. "Here?"

The power he willingly gave over to her made her giddy. "Well, that's pretty good, but it won't do the job, I think."

His hands dipped down, past her waist, over her abdomen, cupping her intimately. "Here, then?" His voice had grown deeper, unsteady.

"If you do that, we'll never get this dress off."

"Do you want me, Moira?"

She turned in his arms, aching where his hand had been. "Do you love me, William?"

He rained kisses from one cheek to the other, lingering at the corners of her mouth, her eyes. "You did not understand that this morning?"

She barely heard him.

"When I explained to you that joining our kingdoms means nothing to me without you by my side?"

Coherent thought was fleeting. "I..."

"You thought perhaps that I was still trying to convince you to marry me?"

"Well..." She wished he'd kiss the corner of her

eye again. It made her knees weak, and she was tired of standing up with him.

"We are married now, Moira. You are my wife."

"Oh, yes," she agreed on a sigh. She tipped her head to the side just a little, until his lips landed where she wanted them.

"I want to make love to you until the sun rises."

It wasn't the answer to her question, but she was rapidly losing interest in talking. It would have to be enough, for now, that she loved him. "If you don't start on those buttons soon, we won't get to bed until the sun rises."

He chuckled and said, "Pay attention, my love," then slipped her open gown off her shoulders.

"Oh." She was warm from dancing, hot from his hands, and the air felt cool on her skin. She let him push her dress down over her hips, let it crumple on the floor. The French ladies would die, and she couldn't care less.

He stripped off her slip, slid a finger beneath one garter and snapped it playfully, then sucked in his breath. "Your turn."

"You're wearing something I should snap?"

"I am wearing something you should remove."

"A sword, for one."

"You do not like my sword?"

His eyes were pools of blue fire, and she held no illusion that they were discussing a piece of steel. Her fingers grew clumsy with buttons and buckles and hooks, and the zipper of his fly. While she struggled with each one of them, William nuzzled her neck, nibbled her ear and nudged her through his apartment, room by room, inch by inch, until she felt the high mattress against the back of her thighs.

There was little left between them, and he elected to shed his last covering. When she reached behind her to unhook her strapless bra, he pulled her hands forward and kissed her knuckles.

"Not yet." He dimmed the lights, then lifted her to straddle his body. He was hard against her, yet he took his time stretching them out on the silky sheets.

His hands caressed every inch of her flaming skin, and she was beyond caring when he discarded her bra or anything else. It seemed the more impatient she got, the more she wanted him now, the more he practiced patience. She thought he was trying to drive her mad before he finally claimed what she offered. So, in one brief moment of rational thought, she forgot about herself and focused on giving him everything she could. Her hands grew bold on his body. She whispered hot nothings in his ear. She tightened every important muscle in her body.

Her reward was his. Whether the sun came up, that day or any other, was immaterial. If it were up to her, they'd never get out of bed again.

THE SUN DID COME UP. Chloe had no idea when, because it was quite high in the sky before she opened her eyes. William was curled around her, shielding her with his body even in sleep. She planted a soft kiss on his cheek, slid out of bed, slipped into the new silk robe she found in the closet and ordered breakfast. Her hoarded supply of pop-ups was at Castle Ennsway, which was just as well, because she didn't think William would appreciate them.

She roamed the apartment while she waited for coffee and juice. She hadn't gotten much of a look at it the other day, trying as she was to stay out of his bed at the time.

On William's desk, she found a spreadsheet dealing with his plans for unification. If it had been scientific, she'd have had a good chance at understanding it. If it had been artistic, she might have grasped it. But it was accounting, pure and simple, and she hadn't a clue.

Humphrey appeared at her shoulder. "May I have a word, Your Majesty?"

"Yes. What is it?"

"Your friend would like to see you."

Chloe was sure she gave him a blank look.

"Miss Chloe Marshall."

"She's here? Now?" She couldn't believe it. A few hours sooner, and Moira could have been at Chloe's wedding after all.

"Yes, Your Majesty. She has requested to see you immediately. She's waiting in the tower."

"What's she doing there?"

"She says secrecy is of the utmost importance."

*Something must have gone wrong.* "Is she all right?"

"She seems…distracted."

"Let me get some clothes on."

"Remember, Your Majesty," Humphrey warned as she headed for the bedroom, "she doesn't want anyone to know she's here."

Moira's insistence on secrecy obviously stemmed from her not knowing William knew the truth. Had something gone wrong with her new job at the dude ranch? Had she blown her identity? Were paparazzi following her, vying for an opportunity to expose them both?

William snored softly as Chloe pulled on jeans and

a T-shirt and shoved her feet into a pair of sneakers.
She wouldn't disturb him with this until she knew what
was going on.

WILLIAM YAWNED and stretched. Now would be a
good time to tell Moira he loved her. No stress. No
pressure. No adrenaline to blame. No thought that he
was telling her only to get her into bed, because that
was now moot.

He rolled over and opened his eyes to find Moira's
side of the bed empty, then listened to hear what had
wakened him. The footman made no effort to tiptoe
around the apartment as he set up breakfast.

William listened for the shower and heard nothing.
He slid out of bed, put on his robe and went to hunt
up his new bride and tempt her back to bed.

"Good morning, Your Majesty," the footman said.
"This is what Her Majesty ordered. I hope it's to her
liking."

William peered around, but saw no one else.
"Where is she?"

"Her Majesty? I don't know."

William searched the entire apartment and couldn't
find her. He sent for Emma. "Where is she?" he asked
immediately upon her arrival, some fifteen minutes
later.

Emma took a step back at his abruptness.

"Has she gone riding alone? I forbid that."

Emma laughed. "Oh, Your Majesty, forgive me, but
that would be a big mistake."

He sighed and raked his hand through his hair.
"Have my horse saddled at once."

"She didn't go for a ride."

"Then why did you say—"

"I said you shouldn't forbid her, Your Majesty. Moira grew quite independent in the United States."

"Ah, yes. I know all about that."

"I know you do. So you understand."

"I understand my wife ordered breakfast and is not here."

"Yes, well, the footman mentioned that. As much as it confuses me, it seems she went to meet Miss Marshall."

"Why did she not come here?"

"I don't know."

"Did she leave the castle?"

"I'll find out."

Something was not right. As much as it seemed to confuse Emma, it frightened William. Angered him. Was Miss Marshall, as Emma called her, behind the three attempts on his bride's life? Had she returned to do her harm? It made no sense to him, except that he knew Moira's life had been in danger from the time her father sent for her. And he didn't know who was to blame.

He was dressed by the time Emma got off the phone. "Where are they meeting?"

"No one knows for sure, Your Majesty."

He never should have released his prisoner. There had been no more "accidents" while the man was locked up. And now this. He would find her. And if her friend was up to no good, he'd lock her up and throw away the key.

"Moira, my love, where are you?"

"HUMPHREY, are you sure she's in this tower?" Chloe asked.

They'd trekked in a roundabout way through the entire length of the castle. Humphrey, apparently, knew Baesland Castle intimately, because most of the passages they'd taken hadn't seen light, in any form, in a hundred years.

"Quite sure, Your Majesty. She swore me to secrecy. Be careful, now, the steps are narrow. I'll be right behind you."

"Wait here."

"I'm worried about the steps, ma'am. As soon as you reach the top, I'll come right back down and stand guard."

Chloe climbed the winding newel steps, confident she wouldn't fall backward into Humphrey's arms. Now, if it had been William behind her, she might have pretended to—just to touch him again, to feel his arms close around her body, to find out what it was like to make love in an ancient tower. If Moira hadn't been waiting up above.

Chloe topped the last step, paused to catch her breath, then noticed there was no one there.

"Humphrey, you must have the wrong tower."

*Great! Dancing until two, lovemaking until we passed out from exhaustion—I don't need this exercise, much less climbing another tower.*

She heard an ominous creak behind her, the stuff haunted-house movies were made of. She turned to follow him back down the steps, just in time to get a thick wooden door slammed in her face. "Humphrey!"

His voice was only slightly muffled through the wood. "Sorry, Your Majesty."

She pounded on it with her fists. She kicked it with her foot until she thought she'd broken her toes. "Open this door!"

Nothing. She ran to the windows, which were nothing more than arrow loops cut in stone several feet thick. The room was one small circle. There was no way out other than the door. No one on the ground would hear her if she screamed until she was hoarse.

"Humphrey, open the door at once!" She could hear noises outside. Scratches, maybe. Tapping? "Humphrey?"

Then his voice, quite close, clearer than it had been before. "I've set a rather large explosive, Your Majesty."

She moved backward, away from the door, fruitlessly searching for something to shield her from an explosion. "Why?"

"I have a family. I have to keep them safe. It will be over in a moment, I promise you. I used a short fuse. You won't suffer."

What the hell did he think she was doing now?

"Count to a hundred, if you like."

As much as she tried not to, after beating on the door for several more seconds, she found herself counting. She figured she'd used up about thirty counts.

*Thirty-one. Thirty-two.*

She ran to the closest arrow loop, leaned her shoulders in and judged whether her body would fit.

"And if I could, then where?" she asked thin air. A hundred feet down to what? Cobblestones?

*Forty-nine. Fifty.*

"Moira!" she heard in the distance, far below her in the tower. "Moira!"

"William!" she screamed his name.

She heard him call out to her again, but it sounded farther away. He was going away.

*Fifty-five. Fifty-six.*

"Moira!"

*Sixty-two. Sixty-three.* "I'm in the tower!" *Sixty-five. Sixty-six.* "Oh, my God, William, no! Go back!"

"Moira, are you up there?"

There was no need for both of them to die because of some madman. "William, you have to go away. There's a bomb."

"Moira, I hear you!" He continued to call out to her, and she knew he was climbing the steps in leaps and bounds.

*Seventy-seven. Seventy-eight.*

She grabbed the handle, rattled the door on its hinges, but it wouldn't give. "William, go back down! Get away!"

"It is locked," he said from just outside the door.

"I know. Go on, go!" *Eighty-three.* Who the heck knew if she was counting too fast...or too slow?

"What's this?"

"It's a bomb, you idiot. Get the hell out of here!"

"Moira, move away from the door."

"It won't help. There's nowhere to go. Run!"

"Get away from the door," he said in a tone that, even in her petrified state, reminded her of a lion's roar.

She backed off. A second later, the door cracked.

*Ninety-one.*

It splintered. His foot crashed through the wood, followed by his leg, his body, and then his arms were scooping her up over his shoulder and he was running.

*One hundred.*

The roar deafened her, right up until the second she passed out.

## Chapter Fourteen

William came to in a pile of rubble and dust. He had to brush debris from his head, out of his hair and off his face, before he could safely open his eyes. Sprawled head down on a small, cramped, winding stairway, he could not fathom what the hell he was doing there. He had been in bed with Moira.

A deafening roar echoed within his ears. He started to sit up, hoping that would clear his head and help him make sense of all this mess, then realized the stones beneath him were soft, not hard. Warm, not cool.

"Moira. My love."

He moved carefully, so as not to hurt her—if she was alive. Every movement he made dislodged stones and raised more dust. He blocked them with his hands and his feet before they could smash into her lifeless body. "Moira, can you hear me?"

Ignoring his own cuts and bruises, he lifted himself off her. If anything in his own body was broken, he refused to acknowledge it. She was still. So still. He wedged his back against the wall and pulled her into his lap. He wanted to hold her, to will life back into her. As his mind cleared, he realized he should not have moved her. He felt her neck for a pulse, but found none.

A dull throb in his chest escalated into a sharp, searing pain. He did not have to look down to know that he would see nothing wrong on the outside. It was inside. He had not kept her safe. He had had her father bring her to this country, and he had not been able to protect her. He did not care if the whole world saw the tears that slipped silently down his cheek.

His heart was broken.

"Mmmm…"

"Moira?" When her fingers curled against his chest, he found it possible to laugh and cry at the same time. "Do not open your eyes yet, my love." He brushed every speck of dirt clear before he said, "It is all right now."

Her eyelids fluttered open, and he thought hazel the most beautiful color he had ever seen. He hoped their babies had that color. Not that he wanted to bring any babies into this world until he had dealt with the crazy person responsible for this mayhem.

"You okay?" she whispered.

"Yes, you broke my fall, thank you."

She snickered against his chest, reached up and softly brushed a tear from his face. "Anytime."

He heard footsteps and shouts in the distance, coming closer. His staff.

"Who did this?" He had to know. He had to hunt him down and deal with him.

"Humphrey."

William remembered Patrick swearing he had left Moira's mare, only for a moment, to help her assistant secretary. Humphrey would have had access to the chandelier over her bed, too. Pieces started to fall into place. Not answers, but pieces.

"He said...something about keeping his family safe."

Were others involved? William swore he would find the truth.

"You have a choice, my love."

"Hmm?"

"I can stay here and hold you, or I can go find the bastard who did this to you."

"Hold me."

She was too kindhearted. Perhaps he should not tell her exactly what he planned. "You will not stop me from throwing this one into the dungeon."

"Are you kidding? Throw the key into the moat this time. William..."

"Yes?"

"I'm sorry about your tower."

He could not care less. His tower—his whole castle—meant nothing without her. "You *are* rather hard on the antiques."

CHLOE LET WILLIAM carry her back to their bedroom only because he was so attentive. One time, long ago, he had said he loved her, and she hadn't believed him. Now, his every action said it, and she no longer needed the words. He stood her beside the bed and peeled her clothes off with the utmost care, as if doing so would take her skin with it.

Dust fell all around her feet. "I'm going to take a shower."

"You are going to climb into this bed until the doctor checks you out."

"But I'm all dirty."

"I should never have moved you, but, since I did, you will at least rest quietly until we know you are all right."

"William—"

"Get in that bed." His words were firm, but his voice sounded only of love and concern.

"Make me."

"Do not look at me like that."

"Like what?" she asked with an innocent air.

"Like you are hungry."

"Well, I haven't had breakfast yet."

"I was not talking of food, Moira."

"Neither was I."

He sighed, and she allowed him to ease her into bed, but clung to his hand until he gave in and sat beside her. She curled up against his side, beneath his arm. Emotionally, she wanted to sit on his lap and make wild, passionate love with him to celebrate their safety. Physically, her body ached and burned, and it had nothing to do with her husband's proximity.

"I will have Humphrey locked up by sunset, Moira, but until I find out who else is involved, I am afraid you are not safe. I cannot post a guard by every chandelier, and I have no bomb-sniffing dogs."

She curled tighter into him, sensing that she wasn't going to like whatever he proposed.

"I know how much you like to study and learn things. You like rocks and fossils a great deal. You stare at my art collection as if you plan to paint a masterpiece of your own. Plants and lizards fascinate you."

She had no idea where this was leading, but the steady cadence of his heartbeat beneath her ear soothed her.

"I can send you to any university you want—"

She sprang away from him. "No! Ow!"

"Moira, you must lie still."

He held out his arms in a silent invitation to curl against him again. "No. I'm not going to just curl up and die, and that's what'll happen if you send me away."

"It is for your safety—"

"And what about my heart?"

He looked confused.

"I can't live without you, William."

"It is just until I can catch everyone involved."

"I won't go. Wherever you send me, I'll get on a plane and fly right back here."

He eased himself off the bed, stiffly, and she realized he must be as sore as she. More so.

"Perhaps I can join you in a day or two, once I get everyone organized."

Chloe wondered what Moira had been told when she was sent away. Had she been told her father would join her, or send for her soon? Had she been lied to, as Chloe thought William was doing now?

He kissed the top of her head, the only part of her she'd let him touch. "Pull the sheet up, Moira. I will have breakfast sent to you. Anything you want."

"Strawberry pop-ups."

"Please, my chef would quit first."

She didn't watch him walk out of the room. She couldn't. It hurt too much to love him and know he'd send her away. If someone wanted to kill her so much, they'd find her and try again. Next time, someone else might get hurt. If she didn't leave, it might be William.

It could be worse. He could be killed.

When he was working for her, not against her, Humphrey hadn't impressed her as a dangerous man. He'd said his family was in danger, so she could only assume he'd been coerced into doing what he did. It didn't make her feel sorry for him or like him, but it did make her want to question him. She would, too, as soon as they had him under lock and key.

If he didn't want to provide her with answers, she knew where there was a perfectly good torture chamber, complete with a rack.

IT WAS only a matter of hours before Moira heard that Humphrey had been given a new residence in Baesland Castle's dungeon. When she stooped beneath the lintel and entered it this time, it didn't smell so bad. Not nearly as bad as it ought to, considering where Humphrey had tried to send her with his short-fused bomb. The fact that William's life had been endangered, too, incensed her.

William was safely occupied in a cabinet meeting, along with Louis, so she had no worries that he would come along and stop her from doing what she had to do.

Patrick was on duty.

"I want to talk to Humphrey," Chloe told him.

"Oh, Your Majesty, I don't think His Majesty would allow that."

"Excuse me?"

"Uh, I mean, His Majesty said the prisoner couldn't have visitors."

"I'm not a visitor."

"But—"

"I'm your queen."

He fidgeted from one foot to the other. "Yes, ma'am. I know, ma'am."

"Never mind, I remember the way." As if she couldn't find one cell in this cracker-box prison.

Patrick followed on her heels. "I wouldn't want anything to happen to you, Your Majesty. I asked for this duty, you know."

"Really? Why?"

"Everyone who knows me knows I'd have nothing to do with harming you, ma'am. But I want everyone else to know, too."

Chloe found Humphrey in the third cell—the dankest, darkest corner of the dungeon. "Hello, Humphrey."

"Your Majesty! Oh, thank God you're all right."

*Oh, puh-lease.* "No thanks to you."

"He made me, Your Majesty. I swear. I love my wife, my children. He said I'd never see them again if I didn't get rid of you."

"Who, Humphrey?"

"I can't say."

"You'd better."

"No, I can't. My children, you see. He'll harm them for sure."

"Is he holding them somewhere?"

"No."

"Does he have someone else watching them?"

"I don't know."

Her own fuse was growing short. "Well, are you

just going to sit in there and worry about them, or are you going to do something about it?"

Humphrey stood up, and Chloe saw that he was in chains. "I'm scared."

Her eyebrows rose. "You think this is scary, just wait until Patrick gets you out of there and introduces you to our rack."

Patrick cracked his knuckles and rubbed his hands together with glee.

"No!" Humphrey said. "His Majesty said I had until sunrise to decide."

"Guess again. Patrick, get him out of there."

"Yes, ma'am. I'll get the key." He sounded positively delighted.

It was difficult to see Humphrey's face in the poor light, but his silence told Chloe most of what she needed to know. Above all the ancient odors, she smelled his fear.

"No, no, you can't," he said when Patrick returned.

Patrick took his time flipping through a whole ringful of large keys—as if anyone would believe he needed all of them for only three cells.

"It's not right, I tell you."

"Tell me what I want to hear," Chloe said, "and we won't have to see if I can operate that rack. I've never used one before. I'm afraid my touch won't be too delicate. I'd hate to jerk your arms right off at the start."

Patrick clucked his tongue and shook his head. "That would be a shame, Your Majesty. He might pass out, then we'd have to wait for him to come to before we started all over again."

Chloe looked pensive. "Yes, well, I don't know any other way. Get him out of there and strap him on."

"No!"

"Yes, ma'am."

Chloe's sneakered toe tapped the stone floor while Patrick unlocked the door, unlocked the chains and dragged an unwilling Humphrey out to the rack. Eyes darting rapidly, like a wild animal's, he glanced around, but he didn't seem to like anything else he saw any better.

Chloe stood next to a helmetlike device. "How does this work?"

"That goes over a prisoner's head, ma'am. Then you turn the screws until they drill a hole right through the skull into the brain."

In the dim light, it was difficult to be certain that Humphrey's face turned white.

"Which works better, I wonder?"

Patrick shrugged. "Don't know. We can try one, then the other."

"Louis!" Humphrey screamed. "It was Prince Louis, I tell you!"

"My brother?"

"Yes, Your Majesty. He wanted control of Ennsway. He said as the son, it was his right."

"But it isn't even Ennsway anymore. We've merged with Baesland." Just as suddenly as she said it, she realized that if she and William were killed, Louis would rule the new country. "Oh, dear Lord, he's with William now."

She flew out the door, not caring what Patrick did with Humphrey. She had to get to the cabinet meeting—wherever the hell that was. She had to warn William.

WILLIAM had carefully explained the first stage of unification to his cabinet, seated around the long rectangular table. It was a closed meeting, and he had left strict orders at the door that they were not to be disturbed for anything.

He wanted everything to run smoothly. He wanted everyone in any position of authority to know exactly what was expected of them. He wanted to assure everyone that this was for the betterment of all, and he didn't have any problems there.

And then he wanted to go find his bride and tell her he loved her, over and over again, so that she would never doubt it.

"Does everyone understand what is expected?"

They nodded in unison.

"Then, on to stage two."

A footman appeared at his side. "Your Majesty, Her Majesty, the Queen, wishes to speak to you."

The doctor had assured William that she was all right, would just be uncomfortable for several days. "Tell her I will be another hour."

The footman stood his ground. "I did, Your Majesty."

William, willing the footman away, glared at him for this needless interruption.

He held out a note instead. "She said to give you this."

William tucked the note into his pocket.

"She said to stand here until you read it."

William drew himself up to his full height. "You

have an undying urge to rebuild my tower single-handedly?''

"No, Your Majesty. But I heard Her Majesty has been experimenting in the torture chamber, and I would rather rebuild the tower.''

William could not help himself—he smiled. It would be just like Moira to hunt through the library until she found an explanation of how each device worked, then try them out for herself. He opened and read the note, which requested to speak to him immediately.

"Please tell Her Majesty that I have received her request, and that I will meet with her in one hour."

"Yes, Your Majesty."

"And since she is well enough to run about the castle, see to it that there are men-at-arms to protect her."

"Right away, Your Majesty."

William thought that would be the end of that. When he was finished, he would have to explain to Moira that she could not disturb him in his meetings, that she could not threaten the footmen with torture in order to have them bow to her orders over his. Though she had done it quite creatively.

"Where was I? Oh, yes. Stage two will begin with— What the hell is that racket?"

All heads turned toward the door, where it was quite obvious that Moira, outside, wanted to get inside.

"Louis, sit down. We will continue."

But Louis did not sit down. He strode toward William, at the head of the table.

The door flew open and smacked back against the wall. Moira, hair flying and eyes sparking, pointed toward the center of the room and shouted, "There he is! Seize him!"

*Oh, my, she has a head injury.*

"Footman, send for the doctor."

Moira wheeled on the men-at-arms. "Seize Prince Louis at once, or I'll see you all in the torture chamber for a little fingernail-pulling party."

"Louis?" William asked in surprise. He was even more shocked when the young prince flew at him, and was spurred into motion when he glimpsed a blade of steel aimed at his chest.

A quick dodge on his part, followed by half a dozen men-at-arms tackling the prince, and William abandoned stage two for the moment.

"What is the charge, Your Majesty?" one of the cabinet members asked.

"Attempted assassination."

William looked down at Louis's face, difficult to see as it was pressed into the floor, then back at Moira. "You are certain?"

"Humphrey confessed."

"To whom?"

"To me. I've sent guards to his home to protect his family in case Louis has other accomplices."

William frowned. "Humphrey would tell me nothing."

Moira grinned. "So he said. But I have my ways."

"So I heard." For someone who was new to being royal, she had brought along a certain American sassiness that allowed her to adapt quite well. Maybe too well.

"What will you do with him?" he asked as Louis was dragged away.

"Exile him to a small, remote island somewhere." She addressed everyone in the room then. "Excuse the interruption, please. I know His Majesty would like to get back to whatever y'all were doing."

"I was going over the plans for merging our two countries."

She nodded, as if in agreement.

He turned to his cabinet and drawled most effectively, "If *y'all* will excuse me, I'm fixin' to go consult with my new queen on a few matters before we continue. Say, tomorrow?"

There were grins and nods and disguised elbow-jabbing as William approached Moira and crooked his elbow and they left arm-in-arm.

"I thought you had everything worked out," she said. "I saw your spreadsheet, and I'm afraid I can't be of much help there."

He stroked the back of her hand with one fingertip. "We will not be going over any spreadsheets."

"Oh?"

"We will be going over...other business."

"Such as?"

"Well, for one, my chef has come up with some pastries he would like you to sample. I thought I would help."

"Strawberry?"

"I told him nothing else would do. I hope that is all right. And then..." He ran his finger over the sensitive spot where her index and middle finger joined.

"Then what?"

Over and over, he stroked, while he waited for her to get his point.

"William?" She looked up at him, and light dawned in her eyes. She smiled shyly. "Oh. I see. Well, I don't know. I'm not very good at this business stuff. We may have to go over it again and again.''

''All day?''

''Absolutely.''

''And all night?''

''Definitely.''

''And you will believe me when I tell you I love you?''

''I already do.''

He raised her fingers to his lips and kissed them. ''Ah, Moira, you are one hell of a queen.''

# Epilogue

*On a tiny, remote tropical island*

Under darkness of night, Louis boarded a chartered jet.

"Where to?" the pilot asked.

"Just get up in the air, and then I'll tell you."

"Hey, look, buddy—"

"Do it!"

The pilot held up his hands to signify no further argument. "Sure. Calm down."

Louis didn't want anyone knowing until the last possible moment that he was headed for the United States. There, somewhere, was his real sister, the woman who had duped him out of his crown.

For that, she would pay.

* * * * *

*Want to find out how Princess Moira*

*handles a hunky Colorado cowboy?*

*Don't miss the sequel*

*in this Princess & Pauper duet:*

# *COWGIRL IN PEARLS*

*by Jenna McKnight*

*American Romance #724*

*April 1998*

WHEN CHLOE MET
Princess Moira back in college,
she only had dreams of meeting a
suave, sexy king. When Princess Moira
met Chloe, she could only dream of
meeting a hunky, honest-to-God cowboy. But
then the oddest thing happened: they switched
places. They thought it would be easy, just for a
little while, to see how the other half lived.
But they couldn't have been more wrong....

# Jenna McKnight

*brings you all the
hilarious highjinks in
a very special duet.*

### Don't miss

March 1998—
**#719 PRINCESS IN DENIM**

April 1998—
**#724 COWGIRL IN PEARLS**

Available wherever
Harlequin books are sold.

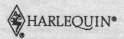

## Catch more great
# ◆ HARLEQUIN™ Movies

### featured on the movie channel tmc

Premiering March 14th
***Treacherous Beauties***

starring Emma Samms and
Bruce Greenwood based on the
novel by Cheryl Emerson

Don't miss next month's movie!
*Hard to Forget*
based on the novel by bestselling
Harlequin Superromance® author
Evelyn A. Crowe, premiering
April 11th!

If you are not currently a subscriber to
The Movie Channel, simply call your
local cable or satellite provider for more
details. Call today, and don't miss out
on the romance!

*100% pure movies.*
*100% pure fun.*

◆ HARLEQUIN™
*Makes any time special.*™

An Alliance Television Production

# He's every woman's fantasy, but only one woman's dream come true.

For the first time Harlequin American Romance brings you THE ULTIMATE...in romance, pursuit and seduction—our most sumptuous series ever. Because wealth, looks and a bod are nothing without that one special woman.

# THE ULTIMATE...

## Pursuit

#711 ~~SHE'S~~ *They're* THE ONE! by Mindy Neff
January 1998

## Stud

#715 HOUSE HUSBAND by Linda Cajio
February 1998

## Seduction

#723 HER PRINCE CHARMING by Nikki Rivers
April 1998

## Catch

#729 MASQUERADE by Mary Anne Wilson
June 1998

# Don't miss these Harlequin favorites by some of our top-selling authors!

| | | | |
|---|---|---|---|
| HT#25733 | THE GETAWAY BRIDE | $3.50 U.S. | ☐ |
| | by Gina Wilkins | $3.99 CAN. | ☐ |
| HP#11849 | A KISS TO REMEMBER | $3.50 U.S. | ☐ |
| | by Miranda Lee | $3.99 CAN. | ☐ |
| HR#03431 | BRINGING UP BABIES | $3.25 U.S. | ☐ |
| | by Emma Goldrick | $3.75 CAN. | ☐ |
| HS#70723 | SIDE EFFECTS | $3.99 U.S. | ☐ |
| | by Bobby Hutchinson | $4.50 CAN. | ☐ |
| HI#22377 | CISCO'S WOMAN | $3.75 U.S. | ☐ |
| | by Aimée Thurlo | $4.25 CAN. | ☐ |
| HAR#16666 | ELISE & THE HOTSHOT LAWYER | $3.75 U.S. | ☐ |
| | by Emily Dalton | $4.25 CAN. | ☐ |
| HH#28949 | RAVEN'S VOW | $4.99 U.S. | ☐ |
| | by Gayle Wilson | $5.99 CAN. | ☐ |

(limited quantities available on certain titles)

| | |
|---|---|
| **AMOUNT** | $ _____ |
| **POSTAGE & HANDLING** | $ _____ |
| ($1.00 for one book, 50¢ for each additional) | |
| **APPLICABLE TAXES*** | $ _____ |
| **TOTAL PAYABLE** | $ _____ |

(check or money order—please do not send cash)

To order, complete this form and send it, along with a check or money order for the total above, payable to Harlequin Books, to: **In the U.S.:** 3010 Walden Avenue, P.O. Box 9047, Buffalo, NY 14269-9047; **In Canada:** P.O. Box 613, Fort Erie, Ontario, L2A 5X3.

Name: _____

Address: _____ City: _____

State/Prov.: _____ Zip/Postal Code: _____

Account Number (if applicable): _____

*New York residents remit applicable sales taxes.
Canadian residents remit applicable GST and provincial taxes.

Look us up on-line at: http://www.romance.net

075-CSAS

HBLJM98